The Monster Mayhem & Magical Love

Lawrence H. Sola

Black Rose Writing | Texas

ISBN: 978-1-68513-253-8
PUBLISHED BY BLACK ROSE WRITING
www.blackrosewriting.com

Printed in the United States of America
Suggested Retail Price (SRP) $20.95

The Monster Mayhem & Magical Love is printed in Palatino Linotype

*As a planet-friendly publisher, Black Rose Writing does its best to eliminate unnecessary waste to reduce paper usage and energy costs, while never compromising the reading experience. As a result, the final word count vs. page count may not meet common expectations.

For Lauren and Jerry
Life is an adventure
Love and laugh

Even after a heartbreaking cry

ACKNOWLEDGEMENTS

To Gregory—thanks for your boundless enthusiasm and insightful editing. It was a pleasure to work with you again.

To everyone who inspired characters that made this book series.

To the bookworms who have supported me in so many ways.

To Reagan and the talented staff at Black Rose Writing.

To my loving mother, Jo Ann, for providing a cozy writing office.

To We the People, ensuring the government gets all of its powers from the Citizens of the United States of America.

To those who have shared heart-wrenching stories of mental illness and addiction. Since the onset of the pandemic, there have been various impacts on societal well-being. The diseases of despair have spiked cases of mental illness and substance use disorders like no other time in history. I hope this story provides strength to those suffering in silence. You are not alone.

To Allison, I am forever grateful for our magical love.

The Monster Mayhem & Magical Love

CONTENTS

PROLOGUE

JANUARY 14, 2020

Life was good.

I felt quite the enchanted man sipping my coffee on this Tuesday morning. I could look back on twenty-seven months of trials and tribulations and see a trail of love. Our fitness center was doing well, and the upcoming release of my new novel, *The Gym,* granted me an auspicious interview with a prestigious book magazine.

With Saturday's interview in my thoughts, I was eager to add an epilogue to the sequel that would capture that afternoon while intertwining the third installment to my book series. I refused to question why that interview stirred something inside me, but it had.

I sat, opened a new notepad, and wrote: *The editing and production stage for the manuscript is underway. I was interviewed by Carla Kimbrel, a Gator alum who worked for Book Buzz Magazine. With the novel's release date only months away, it went without saying that I was excited. Ironically, our paths crossed when Carla, friends with none other than Michelle "Cruella" Crowley, suggested she interview me. It felt like another serendipitous encounter.*

I looked up from my notepad.

My fiancée, Allison Tinke, scampered through the kitchen in a white button-down blouse and panties. She glanced over her shoulder at me and opened the French doors. I felt a chill that had nothing to do with the cool air rushing in with the morning breeze. She stepped out on the lanai, slipped on dress slacks drying on a chair, and hurried back in looking like Elizabeth Halsey in *Bad Teacher*. Her lips curled up at the corners.

"I didn't sleep well," she said, shutting the doors. Her voice was stiff.

"Guilt will do that," I said, standing up. "So, how's that doctor you dated?"

She managed not to wince. "You mean Shawn Avery?"

My head tilted to the side. "Yes," I said slowly. "Doctor Strange."

"He's stressed out. Can you call my phone?"

I marched into the family room on the third ring. "It's silenced," I huffed, pointing to the spot on the couch where she had been curled up. "But you were right there." Her hands slid under a cushion, fishing for it. "Until one in the morning."

Allison straightened up remorsefully. "It wasn't that late," she said, thinking. Then, with a few quick steps to her desk, my favorite educator sifted through some papers scattered over a textbook and waited for my response. Slowly and deliberately, I told her she should have come to bed. She nodded and moved toward the coffee table. Within steps of it, she noticed her phone under it and snatched it up. "Shawn believes an engineered virus that leaked from a bioweapons lab will cause a global pandemic." She paused, looking at me. "Do you think that's possible?"

"Yes, in Hollywood," I said, with more than a hint of sarcasm. "The movie was called *Contagion*."

Her unease intensified, scrolling through Dr. Strange's texts. "Here it is," she continued and began reading them: "A growing number of American elites quietly believe that the Chinese totalitarian regime is superior to American democracy. Many of them are willing to sacrifice American security for personal enrichment. In other words, hidden agendas are funding gain-of-function research. It alters a disease to increase transmissibility. This virus was designed in a lab to attack humans. My contact warned me that malice was involved in this leak. I fear this virus will wreak havoc around the world."

With raised eyebrows, I said, "And you didn't marry this ray of sunshine?"

"Larry, I'm nervous. The virus is spreading rapidly. They might enforce a mandatory lockdown in Wuhan."

"China?"

"Yes." Her chin lifted to me. "The lab is in Wuhan, China. Shawn's contact was very involved in the activities of that lab."

I turned on the TV. There was no mention of this madness on any of the news channels. When I cleared my throat, waiting for an explanation, she recalled how CNN reported a mysterious pneumonia outbreak in Wuhan the week before. I refocused on her face in time to meet her hardening eyes.

"Allison, there's nothing about any lab leak, virus, or lockdown."

She brushed a pesky strand of blonde hair from her pretty face. "Shawn swore this proves that there's a cover-up. You need to read what he wrote." She handed me her phone. "Quick, my battery is dying." I glanced at his texts, relieved they were free of any heart emojis, and then the screen went dark.

"I've seen enough," I said, shaking my head.

"What does that mean?"

"I'm wary of anyone who writes a mile-long text without one emoji."

"Shawn writes research papers, Larry," she continued, increasingly irritated. "Real literature: Not fairy tales with pixie dust, piggyback rides, and ponytails!"

"It sounds like you're leaving my sacred Never Land for Doctor Strange's mysterious enclave."

Allison couldn't help it; she finally laughed. "Can you ever be serious?" Then, with a deep breath, she put her hands on her hips and stated: "You had a Wendy and a Tinker Bell in consecutive storylines and should know that most facts can be stranger than fiction: Our love story is proof of that."

"Please don't compare our magical moments with this guy's midnight melodrama," I said, returning her phone.

Allison's blue eyes clouded in a struggle for comprehension, and she wanted to change the subject. She glanced back at my notepad. "Your book interviewer's texts are more absurd than Shawn's," she said, walking me to the front door. "Did you tell CARLA she does not have carte blanche to ongoing questioning?"

My gaze shifted to the sun's morning rays, moving across my converse sneakers. "No, but I will," I assured her, checking the time. "I'll call you later." I grabbed hold of the door. When I turned to Allison with a smile, she was already smiling back at me. "I love you."

"I love you more," she said softly. "I'm sorry, I overreacted."

"Me too," I replied, casting a last glance at her before shutting the door behind me.

I pondered greatly en route to our beloved beachside fitness center, which inspired my upcoming novel. I opened the windows as a hazy sunrise lifted over the Atlantic. Although the brisk salty air instilled optimism for the year ahead, I could not deny that Allison had a point about Carla Kimbrel. When I stopped at Ocean Avenue's light, I took an unsettling breath as a new text from Carla flashed up: The Monster had Captain Hook terminate my boss after our election piece exposed something much darker!

I had no idea what she'd meant. I gripped my phone and read her follow-up: I want you to write this story. Can you talk?

Minutes blurred by, and then Carla called me the instant I spun my wheel into The Gym's parking lot. Although my conscience screamed out that Captain Hook had flexed his political muscles again, I sensed there was more to this. I answered with an anxious hello, and she cut me off. "My trips to D.C. have unearthed a shocking global conspiracy that has collided with your fairy tale. When can we meet?"

"I'd love to hear more," I said wearily. "But my publisher wants a continuation of the love story with characters from *The Gym*, not the White House—"

"This one has both. Do you remember Caroline, the pharmaceutical rep from D.C. who came to The Gym with her boyfriend, who looked like George Costanza?"

I twitched. "Why do I feel like I'm having amnesia and déjà vu at the same time?" My thoughts raced back to the interview when Carla mentioned flying to a D.C. fundraiser that night. I was suspicious but also very much intrigued. "How do you know Caroline?"

"She's dating The Monster—my ex-husband, Stuart Grossman."

I had to have heard her wrong.

I cleared my throat. "The tech tycoon from Seattle?"

"Yes. Stuart set his sights on Congress but became Hook's business partner instead."

"Why?"

"He had to silence his scientist brother who lived in Florida. After charming his way into Hook's inner circle, Stuart set his brother up with Hook's ex, Michelle Crowley."

I felt my mouth drop open. "The Michelle I renamed Cruella in my book?"

"Yes. When Stuart discovered they all made your last storyline, he became paranoid. Soon after, he had Michelle suggest I interview you so he could read the manuscript."

"What's he paranoid about?"

"The heinous acts he committed in the background of that storyline," she replied hastily. "I'll explain when we meet." Carla paused with voices in the background. And then she shouted at them, "I know the risks involved—I don't care." I gripped my phone tighter, listening intently: Her voice was frantic. "That man-made catastrophe has changed everything—"

A loud voice interrupted her. "Carla, he will use his power and influence to ruin your reputation. This election scares me. This story isn't worth your life."

"This story is paramount!" she cried, "Our hopes and dreams will be lost if the lies aren't exposed—if the monsters aren't defeated." There was silence, and then Carla said, "Larry, are you there?"

"No!" I blurted out. "I don't want to write about any monsters."

"You must," she insisted. "I'll explain why when I see you. I'm dating an infectious disease doctor who knows the truth. His friend at the FBI wants to review what we wrote, but my boss fears it will only put the whistleblowers in danger."

"What are you saying?"

"We live in a time where honest doctors and scientists are silenced, so corrupt politicians and the evil elite can gain more control. It is truly criminal." I considered Dr. Strange's forewarned cover-up. Before I could explain it, Carla went on, speaking with cold contempt. "If you can stomach a real mess of corruption, I'll show you the makings of a dark fairy tale. Do you still use notepads for your stories?"

"I do."

"Well, this story will undoubtedly fill your new notepad with the best material you've ever had."

From my knapsack, I yanked it out.

"Give me a second," I said, scribbling on the second page: *Book #3 - A Global Conspiracy - An election year - Whistleblowers - Caroline - The Monster/Stuart (Carla's ex) - Captain Hook - A real mess of corruption - A Dark Fairy Tale....* "Okay, go on—"

"Do not trust Caroline Haines!" Carla snapped.

I circled Caroline's name. "I doubt I'll ever see her again."

"You will," Carla whispered, "I'll explain when we meet—" a door slammed.

"Carla?"

"Your interview will be out next Tuesday. Best of luck."

I glanced at my phone screen.

The call ended.

CHAPTER ONE

ALL FAIRY TALES SHOULD HAVE A MONSTER

JANUARY 15, 2020

THE GYM

It was a long morning.

Carla came in and out of my mind often. For some reason, I could see chapters forming around her dark fairy tale. Since my life inspired my novels, I wondered if life would throw me another curveball. How could a magical love story collide with an evil, elite monster's mess of corruption?

Indeed, that book couldn't be titled, The Wedding.

What was I missing?

I sat in my office chair, inundated by troubling thoughts.

What heinous acts did this monster commit in the background of my last storyline?

Did Carla's election piece expose Dr. Strange's lab leak?

Why was Allison even talking to him?

Could I be subconsciously internalizing something else?

With a sigh, I glanced at the clock. It had been twenty-four hours since I'd heard from Carla. Until yesterday, it felt like she'd text me every twenty-four minutes. I thought about calling her again. Instead, I welcomed a new group of yoginis to The Gym.

Somehow, in the mix was one of Carla's gossipy coworkers. She knew I was a writer Carla interviewed and seemed determined to tell me exactly what I needed to hear. As she walked and talked, I followed her to the yoga studio, listening intently; I was increasingly intrigued.

Minutes later, as she unrolled her yoga mat, I thanked her and hurried back to my new notepad. I opened it, took a calming breath, and captured every word.

Conversation notes - 1/15/2020 - Even at nearly forty, Carla felt that life should be a little crazy. She was a free spirit consumed by wanderlust and, more specifically, adventures with charming men. Although Carla had only published political pieces through her magazine, she had plans to write an adult fairy tale inspired by her life. As this gossiper insisted it was the reason Carla interviewed me, she pulled up her latest Instagram post with a disturbing illustration of a dead girl. Carla wrote: Fairy tales were never meant to be just sweet stories with little substance. From an early age, they intended to teach us that monsters exist. Fairy tales show us that these evil creatures can be defeated. That is the power of a story. That is the power of fairy tales.

We were meant to meet.

With Carla's voice in my ear, I added: *This story is paramount. Our hopes and dreams will be lost if the lies aren't exposed–if the monsters aren't defeated!*

Dr. Strange believed someone was willing to sacrifice American security for personal enrichment.

Could this lab leak have happened?

I couldn't take it anymore. I grabbed my phone to call Carla and looked at the screen. I had a missed text from my youngest beta-reader, Ashley Grove: Do you remember my psychic reading that predicted 2020 would end an innocent time?

I took a breath, held it, and read her explanation: Last night, I dreamt that you wrote the story that ended this era after losing everything. I know it's crazy, considering you're living a blissful fairy tale, but I can't remember having such a vivid dream.

I exhaled, visualizing her dark brown eyes, focusing on her screen as she hit the arrow. The beautiful brunette sent many harried texts from The Gym over the past nine months. It was endearing how she looked out for her family and friends. And I had looked out for her as if she was my daughter.

Ashley joined the fitness center last spring after receiving her MLIS from UNC. The aspiring librarian would come in a few times a week, work out with light weights, and then walk on a treadmill while immersed in her kindle. After reading my first novel, *The Show*, the twenty-six-year-old volunteered to critique book number two, *The Gym*. She had become a fixture at the fitness center ever since.

Ashley's texts typically amused me, but this morning overwhelmed me. I shifted uncomfortably, needing a moment when her concerns continued: I cried because it all happened in the coming weeks. I just need you to tell me I'm overreacting.

This is crazy.

Now, three people believed something terrible would happen. And soon. I decided to text Carla first: **Did you plan on explaining this dark fairy tale?** I hit the arrow too fast, impatience seeping from every pore. I sent a follow-up: **I hope you're okay. Please call me when you can.**

I shook my head. I felt like a fool standing there, breathing too hard, unable to stop dwelling on this. I heaved a long sigh and meandered outside for some fresh air. The sun, hidden partially by clouds, was high in the sky over the fitness center's bustling plaza. I drew an uneven breath, knowing my members were worried about me. I could tell it in their sideways glances and heard it in the way they whispered as they passed.

I googled current viruses and read that an epidemiological team from Beijing arrived in Wuhan to investigate the epidemic. With my elbows on my knees, I leaned forward, holding my phone: I was craving answers.

Moments later, it rang. I jolted upright, expecting it to be Carla, but it was my treadmill dealer.

I moaned, "Good morning, Stan."

"Don't sound so excited."

"I'm sorry. I was expecting someone else. How are you?"

He laughed. "Not as good as you."

I winced.

He continued, "Your new Cardio Elite will be here on Friday."

"That's great."

"Well, my wife complained there weren't enough treadmills for all your new members."

I pushed myself off the bench. "Thank her for me, Stan," I said, walking back into The Gym.

"You bet, Larry. Cheers to the fitness center, your book, and your lovely fiancée."

"Goodbye, Stan," I said quickly — Then I heard voices rumbling over the U.S. – China trade deal.

As I entered the office, I glanced back at three young couples staying at a bed and breakfast up the road. The Texas natives had purchased day passes while scowling at CNN from the spin bikes. Then, the most outspoken one said, "China creates an Orwellian dystopia for their people, commits genocide against ethnic minorities, and this fake news network defends them while questioning our President."

With murmurs of agreement and whispers of contempt, his wife turned to me. "Excuse me, sir," she said. "Can you please change it to Fox News?"

I nodded, surveying the cardio area.

Nancy Neiman's posture was rigid with tension. The staunch Democrat's hands were in her lap, clasped in a death grip as she sat on a rowing machine behind them. Her friends shook their heads, but I sensed Nancy was about to blow. Despite the gravity of the situation, I retreated to the office, texting Ashley: **Don't worry about those psychic readings. I can't talk now. Crazy morning. I'll catch you up later. Just stop crying, ya silly goose.**

The lady requesting the channel change entered the office. "I'm sorry to keep bothering you," she said. "We're not racists. We have issues with anyone who forms this moral superiority complex when it comes to having discussions about politics." She paused and glanced back at Nancy. "Everything is great right now, and we'd appreciate a real news update about this important election."

Everything is great right now.

I smiled, snatched the remote off the desk, changed the channel, and apologized to the group.

In unison, they said, "Thank you."

Nancy was staring at them as though committing their faces to memory. Then, she shifted her gaze to me. "Larry," she snapped loudly. "May I speak with you?"

Straightening, I choked out, "Sure." Gripping the remote, I headed her way.

Nancy's eyes narrowed at me through her gold-rimmed glasses. "I guess you want me to watch the Stuart Grossman interview at my house?"

That's The Monster!

At that moment, everything I wanted to say became irrelevant. My adrenaline took over. "He's the tech titan, right?"

"Stuart Grossman is a caring philanthropist looking to get into politics," she said. "He would make an excellent President. Of course, he's a Democrat." She paused, shaking her head at me. "Why are you catering to those rude Republicans?" Her voice was barely above a whisper. "You're never going to see them again." I pinned on my overtly patient smile, the one that silently called the person asking a silly question an idiot. But Nancy had grown accustomed to that and only became further infuriated. She checked her watch. "Just know we will not support any businesses that back Trump!"

"I understand, Nancy."

I stood back as she stormed out, complaining that the air was set too high and the music was too loud—all part of her usual routine.

With a calming breath, I greeted Rich, something-or-other, one of my newest members, as he shuffled in. It didn't matter that he began the conversation complaining about Nancy. What kept me engaged was that he knew Stuart Grossman.

Rich worked closely with Stuart at Hook's firm. He swore The Monster's connections to Beijing's highest levels of power had become a calling card for prospective investors. It was the reason Hook had been so tolerant of Stuart's profoundly troubling relationship with the Chinese regime. I glanced at The Monster's CNN interview as Rich told me that Stuart's ties to China had gone back to his Silicon Valley days when he made his fortune.

A member watching that interview interrupted our conversation: "Stuart Grossman just called President Trump a criminal."

Another voice said, "Fox News swears Grossman is wicked."

As the members converged under the TVs, I wrote in my notepad: *The media spins a narrative that one's political opponents are wicked or even criminal. It's no longer about debating political views. It's out-party hatred exceeding in-group solidarity. Americans' voting behavior today is driven more strongly by contempt for the opposition than by support for one's own side.*

I saw a correlation to Carla's storyline and sighed as my call to her went to voicemail.

Time stood still.

For the next hour, I pulled up anything I could find about The Monster and added it to my notes: *Stuart James Grossman - Born October 25, 1976, Seattle, Washington - Dropped out of Harvard - Spouse Carla Ann Kimbrel - Married 2015 - Divorced 2017 - no children. News Headline - 11/5/2019*

- Stuart Grossman's Dark Agenda - Grossman has donated massive amounts of money to the World Health Organization and other such entities. While promoting disease control through universal vaccines sounds admirable, critics claim his wealth has influenced the recipients. This claim is worth considering when you look at how WHO's philosophies now mirror Grossman's. Grossman has long been an advocate for vaccines and population control. To the software billionaire, the human condition is just a mathematical formula. Health and prosperity equal resources divided by population. Grossman believes the world's resources are ultimately finite, and the only way to improve things is by reducing the world's population. In 2014, the World Health Organization was accused of the chemical sterilization of Kenyan women without their knowledge. Grossman's plan was a mass sterilization exercise using a proven fertility-regulating vaccine. In 2010, Malaria vaccine trials killed over 150 African infants. In 2005, Grossman-funded operatives working for an anti-meningitis campaign forcibly vaccinated 500 African children. Local newspapers in South Africa wrote: "We are guinea pigs for drug makers!"

I tapped my pen on the page and scribbled:

All fairy tales should have a monster!
Who is this monster - Stuart Grossman?

I stared at his name and vowed I'd find out.

CHAPTER TWO

PLAYING DETECTIVE

JANUARY 21, 2020

THE HOUSE ON RIVERSIDE DRIVE

A week went by with no word from Carla.

That morning, I was skeptical that her enigmatic interview would be published. Today was the day Carla's piece on *The Gym* would be featured in *Book Buzz Magazine*, but I felt more edgy than excited. I spilled my coffee, pacing in the kitchen when Allison hurried in.

"What's wrong?" she asked.

I hesitated. "I don't know where to begin."

Allison placed a bridal magazine on the counter and checked the time. "Well, start somewhere," she said, "I only have a few minutes."

I nodded, took a breath, and began. I told her about everything that had happened, the call, and Carla's ambiguous message. At that point, my fiancée found her way to my notepad. I stopped there, watching her read my notes while wishing I'd closed it. I wasn't prepared to explain why I was writing again. But it didn't matter; Allison knew. "Carla's made an impression on you. I want to hear about this dark fairy tale she sold you." I repeated what Carla had told me, but since I mocked Dr. Strange for saying similar things, Allison only smiled at that, which made me want to scream. I couldn't explain why I hadn't heard from Carla.

Finally, I looked to end the conversation. "Never mind," I said with a sigh.

"No, I heard you on the phone selling an epilogue to your publisher that would bridge the stories," she replied, picking up my notepad. "Please explain this."

"Write's intuition—I don't know, it could be nothing."

"Or book three." She shook her head. "Won't adding an epilogue delay *The Gym's* release?"

"Just a month."

Allison kept staring at me; I felt like a deer in headlights, frozen, unable to look away or move. "Who came up with the Peter Pan Man book series?"

I knew I had to tell her. "Carla."

"I wanted a break from your adventures, Peter. Besides, you promised me that the title of book three would be, *The Wedding*."

Our gazes shifted to her phone when it pinged on the kitchen counter. I passed it to her and noticed Dr. Shawn Avery texted her: **Wuhan is going under lockdown!**

"It's Dr. Strange," I groaned.

She kissed me. "We'll talk later."

"I love you."

"I love you more," she said, rushing out.

I watched Allison drive off. Then I snatched up my keys, beelined to a Walgreens, almost knocked over an unsmiling employee, and approached the magazine section wearily. At first, I couldn't find it, but then I saw the words: *Book Buzz Magazine* behind a copy of *BOOKFORUM*. I pulled it out and gasped at The Monster on its cover. He was a handsome man. With my heart thumping in my chest, I flipped through it as my fears became my reality. My book was omitted.

I hopped back in my car and called Allison to vent. On the third ring, she answered, "I'm preparing for my fifth graders to take a test. Can I call you back?"

"My book didn't make the magazine."

Then, a pause. "Is it because Hook now owns it?"

"I don't know," I said, thinking about The Monster. "There might be more to this."

"After reading your notepad, I'm sure of it," she replied quietly. "But the fitness center's doing well, so stay positive." Her students called to her. "I have to go—"

Click.

This lost opportunity ate away at me during the ten-minute drive to The Gym. I trudged inside, overthinking everything. With Carla's voice still in my ear, I opened my notepad and shook my head. I pulled it back after pushing it to the side, inexcusably obsessed with this dark fairy tale that would impact the world. I picked up a pen and began tapping it on my notepad, reading about Dr. Strange's lab leak and Ashley's psychic reading.

Perhaps they were just crazy coincidences.

Perhaps there was another reason Cruella suggested Carla interview me.

I circled Michelle "Cruella" Crowley's name.

Perhaps.

However, there was only one way to find out. I had to find Cruella. Sitting in the office, I swiveled in the chair, scanning the fitness center for anyone who knew the troubled thirty-something. With no luck, I grabbed my phone and pulled up *The Gym's* manuscript to jog my memory of the last time I'd seen her.

What am I doing?

I frantically scrolled the pages.

This is crazy.

I stopped at chapter twenty-two.

CRAZY!

CRUELLA CROWLEY - JUNE 12, 2017.

It's time to embrace crazy again.

An hour later, I found Cruella's information on an old sign-in sheet with the date in the story: June 12, 2017. It had an old cell number and an affluent address that further intrigued me.

Sometime after lunch, I ended my shift and headed to my car to play detective. I took a right on Riverside Drive and slowed down, approaching what looked like an abandoned house. There were cracks on the long driveway, overgrown bushes by the garage, and a team of landscapers scurrying around the property like ants on ice cream. One waved me forward, so I parked in front of their trucks, hopped out of my car, and verified the address.

I meandered to the property line, not feeling at all like Columbo. With too many workers eyeing me and no other move, I pretended to take a call:

"Hello?" I said, pressing my phone to my ear.

"Hello to you," a raspy voice responded. I turned to the next-door neighbor, who was retrieving a small parcel from his mailbox. I smiled, and the older gentleman smiled back at me. "You look familiar," he said. "Were you friends with the old owner?"

After a slight pause, I answered, "No, but I am looking for someone who might have lived with him."

He stood there for a moment and looked somewhat surprised. "That house has been vacant for nearly three years." I could tell he was making some quick mental evaluation. "What's the person's name?"

"Michelle Crowley."

"Oh...." He pondered this, taken aback. "How do you know her?"

"Well," I replied, contemplating how to word this, "Michelle recently helped me. She used this address on an old sign-in sheet at The Gym some summers back."

He glared at me suspiciously. "Wait...you're the writer who owns The Gym."

I gave him a quick grin. "Yes. I'm Larry. It's nice to meet you."

"Alan...likewise. So, how did that awful woman help you?"

"She set up an interview for the upcoming release of my new novel."

There was a long pause as the man allowed my words to sink in. "Was the interview published?"

I was amused enough to laugh. "So, you do know her."

As it turned out, he stood at that same mailbox the day Cruella moved in. "Her dreadful voice echoed over me when I came to get my mail," the man recalled. "She barked orders at the doctor even as he pulled boxes out of her beat-up Honda." He shook his head. "Steven was a good man."

I shrugged. "Can you tell me anything else about him?

He raised his hand slightly and nodded. "His name was Dr. Steven Grossman. He was a highly respected scientist who worked all the time—the trips to China ruined his marriage. Beth, his wife, divorced him in early 2017. By that spring, Steven informed us that your friend would be moving in. It was a month after his brother introduced her to him." He took a breath and shook his head. "So, there you have it."

"Do you remember his brother's name?"

"Steven's brother is the tech tycoon Stuart Grossman. He's a preening Marxist cloaking himself as a social activist. One barbecue with him, and I knew he could only relate to others as a function of his own needs." The man's mouth turned down, and then he added, "All summer, we watched a cloud over that house get darker and darker. We knew something bad would happen." He sighed. "In August, our instincts were proven right. Steven died in a boating accident. One that sparked endless speculation."

I felt my face go red. "What does that mean?"

He checked his watch—a cue for me to stop asking questions.

"They never found his body," the man said, shuffling back to his driveway. "I would be careful poking around that storyline, Mr. Writer." He left the sentence dangling for a moment, then sighed. "It might be good that you can't find that awful woman." His voice trailed off as he disappeared behind a cluster of tall Areca palms that separated the properties.

I heard thunder in the distance.

When I turned to leave, I noticed a worker hurrying at me from across the yard: I braced myself for more.

He reached out his hand. "Larry," he said as I blinked, startled. "It's Sharky." Sharky, the Justin Bieber look-alike who gifted me a spin bike in *The Gym's* storyline.

The first thing that struck me was how different he looked. He lost weight around his face, especially his temples and jaw. He looked unwell, exhausted, and scared. I nodded, shaking his hand. "Sharky, what a surprise. How are you?"

He sniffled, pulled his hand back, and wiped his nose with his sleeve. "I got the flu bug that's going around." Turning back to the house, he quietly added, "What are you doing here?"

I pulled Michelle "Cruella" Crowley's old sign-in sheet out of my pocket and explained as much as possible. Sharky's bloodshot eyes grew wide when he noticed the address. I could see the worry carved into his face as he acknowledged that he knew Carla and Stuart. After a slow breath, he confirmed what the neighbor shared while suggesting the situation turned into a twisted love triangle with Captain Hook. I thought back to the day Hook made Cruella come to The Gym in their absurd attempt to buy it. The day was vivid in my memory. I could see the date on the page that began that chapter. But when Sharky referred to Michelle as a perfect Cruella, I froze.

"I referred to Michelle as Cruella in my book."

An unexpected smile sprouted on his glum face. "I enjoyed it." He paused reflectively. "You are certainly a man full of hope. How's Allison?"

"She's good." My mind raced on, intrigued. "But how did you read a book that hasn't been released yet?"

With that, he mentioned being friends with Ashley while admitting that she forwarded him *The Gym's* manuscript after critiquing it. Although I didn't speak, the other landscapers mocked him, and Sharky moved us along. "Walk with me. A storm's coming." He pushed a wheelbarrow full of mulch to a flower bed and whispered, "Did Carla tell you that Stuart got Cruella to interview you?"

"Yes," I said, pondering Carla's warning. "Do you know why?"

The sky darkened as Sharky explained that his brother thought Stuart was spooked by something I wrote. It became difficult for him to elaborate as we passed the other landscapers. They shouted out that Sharky was crazy and drunk. After he dumped the mulch in the flower bed, flustered, I asked him about this infamous tech titan.

Sharky's tone instantly sharpened. "Stuart Grossman is pure evil. Carla refers to him as The Monster." We began walking toward the street. "He's Hook's business partner." He peeked back at the house again as if someone was watching him. "I can't talk here."

My mind kept going back to Carla's call. "Why?"

He looked at me for a moment. He wanted to speak his mind but only said, "The Monster." He wriggled his phone from his pocket. Without looking up, he headed to my car, texting someone.

I hurried beside him. "What else do you know?"

Sharky sniffled loudly. "I know my depression has worsened," he mumbled, looking up from his phone. "This is the end of an innocent time."

He sounds like Ashley's psychic.

"Why do you say that?"

"My brother will explain."

I gasped. "Your brother?"

He finished his text and bobbed a nod. "Yes. Everyone at the firm is on edge—there are many rumors and terminations." Sharky winced when his phone pinged. "My brother responded," he said, reading it. "Are you available on Saturday?"

"Yes."

Cautiously, he continued, "11:30. Before the lunch crowd comes in." He glanced at his brother's message again and then back to me. "At Charlie & Jakes."

"Your brother didn't give me a warm and fuzzy feeling when we met in the last storyline."

"That was before he read your book."

"I see." But I didn't see. I didn't know where Sharky was going. My only recollection of his brother was a passing scowl I had written about in *The Gym*.

Sharky saw I looked puzzled and said somewhat reassuringly, "Larry, my brother, will explain everything."

"Okay, but can you tell me more about Stuart?"

Sharky stared blankly at the Indian River as the sun disappeared behind the ominous clouds. "Stuart Grossman is a dangerous man who seeks to control the masses in a Dystopian Society—"

"Sharky!" a gruff voice called from across the yard. "Get back to work."

Sharky nervously wiped his nose on his shirt sleeve again. "I am," he replied, losing his equilibrium.

I took a step toward him. "You don't look well."

"I told you it's just a flu bug," he insisted, squatting next to my car to pick up a pint of Popov that fell from his jacket. "Stuart is the reason Hook's influence now reaches D.C."

Maybe he is drunk.

"Are you sure you're okay?"

He shrugged, falling to his knees, looking like a sad little boy. "What else did you hear about The Monster?" he asked, desperate to change the subject.

I stared down at Sharky with my hand out to him. But when he pushed it away, I answered. "I heard Stuart wants to get into politics."

"Yes," he said, relieved I gave him a moment. "Stuart made his fortune in the tech industry. Lately, he's been spending time with the bureaucrats in D.C. and less time with Hook." With some slow breaths, he added, "Hook's firm is now public. He bought the doctor's house and owned this landscaping company." Sharky's gaze moved up to me as he stood shakily. "My brother fears this is the calm before the storm." He opened my car door. "Shit…it's Stuart."

I twitched.

The Monster!

A silver 718 Boxster sped up to us and slowed as it went by. It was the handsome tech tycoon. He shifted a gaze to me that felt like a weight. Straightening slowly, I watched the car speed up the driveway.

Sharky stumbled backward. "Meet my brother on Saturday."

I swallowed hard. "I'll be there."

CHAPTER THREE

THE ORWELLIAN WARNING

JANUARY 25, 2020

CHARLIE & JAKES

I pulled into a parking spot. I glanced at my dashboard clock: 11:26.

I stepped out into a beautiful seventy-degree Saturday, wavering like a flame. Do I trust Sharky? Why was he so scared? Maybe he really is crazy. Then, to make matters worse, Allison texted me, wondering where I was. I stared at her message, hoping to hear Sharky's brother out before explaining anything else. But in that moment's hesitation, I had doubts about adding the epilogue. The interview that inspired me was a ploy to read my manuscript. Nothing was what it seemed. With a frustrated sigh, I wanted to leave but only tossed my sunglasses on the passenger seat; I couldn't bring myself to move. Then I heard a voice from the restaurant:

"You are meant to be here!" A rangy barback burst out of the bar area.

The sun reflected in my eyes. "Are you talking to me?" I asked, squinting at him.

"No, my girl!" he replied excitedly, adjusting his earbud while gesturing to a Gen Z'er getting out of her car.

I took that as a sign and headed in.

I entered the restaurant, and a hostess whisked me to a table. As I sat down, a young server approached with a bottle of Josh cabernet. I felt like I had stepped back into *The Gym's* storyline.

"Tyler had to make a call," she said, opening the bottle. "He'll be right back."

I nodded. "Thank you."

She poured me a glass. "So, Peter Pan Man, which wine do you prefer, Kim Crawford from *The Show* or Josh from *The Gym*?"

I paused, realizing that she, too, had read my unreleased book. "How did you hear about the Josh wine—" She cut me off with a whimsical look.

"I read, *The Gym*," she whispered.

I smirked. "You must be friends with Ashley Grove."

The server nodded, smiling. "I heard you were meeting Tyler, so I brought my copy of *The Show*," she grinned, "would you sign it?"

"Of course," I said, reading her name tag. "It's nice to meet you, Hannah."

"Likewise," she said, looking past me. "I'll check back with you guys."

I blinked to my side when a man in his late thirties reached out his hand. "Tyler Harrison," he said as I shook it. "Sharky's brother." I immediately recognized him: There was something unforgettable about his glare.

"It's good to see you again," I replied. "We met...sort of, some years ago, at Sand on The Beach."

He flashed a brief smile. "Yes, the spin bike night I read about," he said softly, a note of wonder in his voice. "Sharky was so stoked he could help you that he ordered your wine during our sales meeting."

I nodded solemnly. "Sharky doesn't seem to be doing well."

"My brother's extremely intelligent," he snapped defensively. "He suffers from depression as many brilliant, creative people do. Abe Lincoln, Lady Gaga, F. Scott Fitzgerald, J.K. Rowling." He paused as I leaned back in the booth, taken aback, and quietly added, "He drinks to numb the pain." Tyler took a sip of wine. "But he's fine."

I drew in a slow breath. "So, are you still working for Hook?"

Tyler looked at me, and his icy-blue eyes narrowed slowly. "No," he said, placing his wine glass down. "Much has happened since your last storyline." He swirled it a few times. "I wish I could go back to those days."

Silence settled between us, broken only by the server dropping her hardcover edition of my first novel on the table. I signed it, and as she walked off, I brought up Carla. Tyler quickly acknowledged her interview but claimed he didn't know her whereabouts. I crossed my arms and had trouble finding my voice. "Well, that interview was never published, and Sharky told me you could shed some light on it."

He released his breath in a steady, even stream. "I can. But I must warn you, what I've heard — what I know, is unnerving."

Neither of us spoke.

Neither of us moved.

If I had brought my Star Trek communicator, I'd have Scotty beam me up.

Then I heard my voice, soft and low. "Thanks for the heads up."

And then his voice, softer still. "His name is Stuart Grossman. And I fell in love with his ex, Carla Kimbrel."

I exhaled, not realizing I was holding my breath. "Well, that's a good start."

Tyler bit down on a smile. "I'm sure you've heard of Stuart."

"I'm learning more every day."

"It all began during *The Gym's* storyline," Tyler said. "In January 2017, Carla moved back to Florida after her divorce." He smiled at the memory and placed the napkins on the table, reminiscing as Sharky had done just days before. "She joined the firm in May and caught my eye at Hook's Memorial Day Luau. We flirted like teenagers even though Stuart watched from the bar."

I tried to laugh. "Stuart was there?"

A faint hint of surprise registered on his face. "Didn't Carla tell you he's Hook's business partner?"

"Yes," I replied. "She said he came to Florida to silence his brother."

"Correct. Dr. Steven Grossman was his name. He was an established scientist who looked like how you'd picture an academic. He was more dedicated to science than to his wife. After she left him, Steven began hanging out with Hook at the Yacht Club. He introduced Stuart to Hook in February. By April, Stuart began flying down for the firm's weekend parties." With pain in his eyes, Tyler paused, and with a sharp breath, he added, "Ironically, they became lavish events orchestrated by Hook."

"What was the irony?"

"Hook had to win your villainous Cruella back from Steven after Stuart played matchmaker."

I sat up straighter, recalling Carla telling me Stuart had charmed his way into Hook's inner circle and muttered, "Unbelievable."

Tyler agreed that Stuart first targeted Cruella to make Hook jealous. However, I quickly realized this was part of a more nefarious plot. Tyler admitted they never questioned the tech titan's actions because times were good, and their parties were better. Soon after the Luau, Tyler began dating Carla. She told him that Stuart had been working closely with Big Pharma lobbyists and only visited his brother after hearing Steven co-authored a book about China's obsession with viruses. He had been alarmed by China's database identifying all deadly viruses with pandemic potential. Tyler talked until his throat was dry. After a gulp of water, my heart thumped as he continued, "Steven was deeply concerned that the U.S. infectious disease chief approved the funding for gain-of-function research."

Dr. Strange mentioned gain-of-function research.

I frowned. "Allison knows a doctor who is worried about that."

Tyler nodded solemnly. "Carla does, too. This research experimented on increasing the transmissibility of a virus infecting humans." His voice was purposely soft. He seemed afraid that he'd be yelling if he raised it slightly. "Steven concluded that the research on bat coronaviruses at the Wuhan Institute of Virology was being used to produce a new SAR-like pandemic."

This is Carla's global conspiracy.

After confirming it, Tyler admitted that Carla believed I could write this story as a dark fairy tale with a monster and a prevailing love during a time of pandemonium. When I questioned Tyler, he flinched, and in that tiny expression of pain, I knew something had changed. There was more to say, but Tyler struggled to spit it out. He stopped, took another sip of wine, and said, "Carla's feelings about you are different now. But I'll come back to that after I explain everything."

I hesitated. "Okay, go on."

"Steven predicted China would use this engineered virus to its strategic advantage. At the same time, a core group of elitists manipulates a pandemic to facilitate the largest upward transfer of wealth in history." He paused, knowing I was holding back an eye roll. Then added, "When Steven discovered that Stuart was involved in this plan, he hoped to convince his brother he'd gone too far. Days later, Stuart invited him on Hook's fishing excursion. Steven only went to talk sense into his brother, but he never returned. Dr. Steven Grossman's body was never found, and his book was never published."

My hands rose to my head. "This sounds like a James Patterson novel...."

I watched his face for a reaction, but he certainly didn't show it if he was making this up. He seemed consumed by this story while insisting Steven believed science is about truth, not political correctness. Tyler then explained Stuart's ties to the Big Pharma lobbyists who loathed the President. I kept thinking about Carla's call as the veins in Tyler's neck throbbed. "Stuart endorses big business, more government, and a socialist agenda." He paused and had a faraway look in his eyes. "A pandemic is exactly what The Monster wants—it would close small businesses, kill the economy, and legitimize mandates while their media outlets sell us the biggest vaccine campaign ever. Big Pharma benefits from this culture of corruption, using allies in the administration and Congress to grow their profit margins while everyday people suffer." Finally, he took a breath. "It's sickening."

With questions swirling around in my head, I asked, "What happened after Steven's death?"

"Stuart had Hook promote Carla with the mentality of keeping his friends close and enemies closer."

"Didn't she get money after divorcing a billionaire?"

"Yes, but Carla loves to write. She's always looking for her next story. That fall, the D.C. fundraisers began, and Stuart met Caroline Haines. He charmed her with his sights solely on her Big Pharma connections. Even though Carla hated Stuart, she became increasingly jealous of their relationship. She knew Stuart would bring Caroline to Florida through Hook, ultimately tearing us apart. Stuart was the one toxic man Carla couldn't ignore."

"What happened to you two?"

A lump rose to my throat when Tyler detailed Stuart's corporate restructure of Hook's companies. He swore this only happened because Hook was obsessed with Stuart. "In April 2018," Tyler continued, "Caroline was appointed sales director of RH Marketing Solutions." His voice cracked. "Months later, Carla ended our relationship and took the *Book Buzz Magazine* editor position. She spent her time writing political pieces. By the summer of 2019, Stuart heard Carla was researching Steven's story. In November, Carla began writing it through her own experience. Shortly after, Hook purchased the magazine. Everyone at the firm assumed that Stuart convinced him to buy it to prevent her from writing the story he refused to have exposed. That's when Stuart heard about your book. He became paranoid about a chapter you wrote with Mr. Smee."

My eyes narrowed at him. "Mr. Smee?"

He snatched up his phone. "Chapter Twenty-Two – Cruella Crowley," Tyler said, reading from the manuscript Ashley had forwarded him. "And I quote: It became quickly evident that she had new boobs, a fresh Botox treatment, and was not the slightest bit remorseful Mr. Smee had taken his life." Tyler looked up. "Your Mr. Smee character was inspired by my good friend Connor Lee. He was a brilliant historian who should've been a professor, not a salesman. His brother Lance was a highly credible academic and the co-author of Steven's book. Right after Steven's death, Stuart had his reputation ruined. Lance was labeled an anti-China racist. After losing his job, he became a recluse in the north Georgia mountains, still mourning the loss of his brother and good friend. This brings me back to Stuart's paranoia about what you wrote."

I rubbed my sweaty hands on my jeans. "I'm listening."

"Connor was a staunch Republican who expressed displeasure with Stuart's radical left-wing agenda. He often questioned Stuart's relentless dismissal of their brothers' research. At a business dinner, Connor maintained that Stuart's political views would ruin the American dream—our freedom and the opportunity for prosperity and success."

"He didn't strike me as a guy who confronts anyone."

"Did you ever talk politics with him?"

"No."

"Politics was his passion," Tyler insisted, tapping his index finger on the table. "And when Connor told Hook that Stuart was involved in this pandemic plot, Stuart decided to take matters into his own hands. Stuart's only obstacle back then was Conner Lee. Your books, Mr. Smee, haunted Stuart."

Tyler's statement hung in the air.

"Are you suggesting that his death wasn't a suicide?"

"I'm certain of foul play," he said regretfully. "I believe Stuart drugged him when we were all out. It was a wild night that none of us could recall. When I told Hook that you wrote about Connor's death, Stuart had Cruella suggest your name to Carla so she would interview you—"

"So, you played Stuart to confirm he killed Mr. Smee—" I shook my head "—Connor Lee?"

"It was the reason I told Hook." Tyler kept his face steady. "And the real reason you're here. Behind your little adventure searching for a happily ever after was a disturbing storyline that has collided with you." He paused for a moment and shifted his gaze out the window. "How's your fiancée these days?"

I raised an eyebrow, concerned. "Allison's fine," I said slowly. "Why?"

His gaze turned back to me. "Carla's research of this pandemic story has her working with Dr. Shawn Avery. He's the infectious disease doctor you mentioned earlier: The one who dated Allison."

The remark took a moment to sink in.

"What a small world."

Tyler frowned, and I knew immediately where this was going. "Your fiancée's communication with him is why Carla refused to publish your interview. She no longer believes in your fairy tale."

I was inwardly seething. "Sounds like a woman scorned. Are you sure Carla's not dating him?"

"Of course." His face had gone hard. "I told you she's working with him. Research for the story."

"Interesting." I checked the time. "Well, I appreciate you meeting me here today. Please allow me to pay for the wine."

"No, I want you to understand how serious this cover-up is," he said, shifting away from Carla's beliefs. "It only happens because most of Congress is leveraged, blackmailed, or paid by entities outside the U.S. They answer to someone other than We the People. That is the ultimate issue. And we're all certain to suffer for it. Especially small business owners: I'd look to sell The Gym before it's too late."

As Hannah returned to refill my water glass, I scrutinized him. "Tyler, The Gym had its most profitable year yet." Anger crept into my voice. "I'm sorry. I'm not buying this planned pandemic—"

"You better," he said, cutting me off. "Everything is about to change. The power and greed behind this will alarm every decent Democrat and Republican who cares about democracy, the Constitution, and our children's future."

For a dizzying moment, I couldn't breathe. After calming breaths, I steadied my hand, reaching for my water. Then I spilled some when my phone rang.

Shit.

Allison.

I placed the glass down, lurched for it, took another breath, and answered, "Hey, honey."

"Hey, your notepad is getting scarier by the day. Can you explain this?"

SHIT!

"Well, not really," I said softly, my voice wavering. "I…uh, I'm with someone trying to enlighten me."

"CARLA?"

"No…no, trust me," I pleaded. "Not her."

"Who then?"

"Her boyfriend. Ex-boyfriend. Sharky's brother…Tyler. Anyway, I'll explain at The Fish House tonight. We'll have fun tonight."

"Larry, I'm uncomfortable with Carla's dark fairy tale."

"Don't be. It's nothing that can happen in real life."

Silence.

"I'm going to get my nails done. I'll be back before dinner."

"Sounds good."

Click.

Tyler snapped a glance at the server. "Check, please, Hannah."

She dismissed him with a roll of her eyes.

Tyler sighed heavily and stood up. He wanted distance between us. "Larry, you should read George Orwell's *1984* if you want the rest of this story. I enjoyed *The Gym*." He dropped a fifty-dollar bill on the table, reached out his hand, and I shook it. Walking by me, he added, "I only hope your next book proves me wrong."

I fell back in the booth, disoriented.

Seconds later, I peered over my shoulder, but Tyler was gone.

CHAPTER FOUR

A SCRIPTED VISIT

JANUARY 31, 2020

THE GYM

It was the following Friday. I took Tyler's advice and read George Orwell's *1984*.

WAR IS PEACE.
FREEDOM IS SLAVERY.
IGNORANCE IS STRENGTH.

Those words still sounded in my head days after I finished it. In some twisted way, this dystopian novel, published in 1949, was a stark, haunting glimpse at what could be. From the check-in counter, I observed gym members on treadmills who were glued to the news and scribbled in my notepad:

Humanity is programmed through a TV screen. The idea that truth is arranged through media is our reality. Political language has been designed to make lies sound truthful and murder respectable-George Orwell.

What ifs: What if Carla did confirm a global conspiracy? What if Allison was interested in other men? What if my next book couldn't prove Tyler wrong?

Minutes later, I splashed cold water on my face from a sink in the locker room. I closed my eyes and was further irritated by the periodic drip from the facet. No answers are forthcoming: In other words, I was done thinking about all of it. I dried my face and texted Allison that I loved her. As I entered the yoga studio to check on the new lights, she responded with her typical: I **love you more**!

I grinned, looking up at the electrician. "How are the lights, Tony?"

"We're almost done," he said in a husky voice. "These aren't cheap, but they'll cut your electric bill." He came down from his ladder, flipped the switch, and the room lit up brighter than ever. "What do you think?"

"It's a big difference," I replied. "Great job."

He gave me a small smile—as if he was grateful for the job. "I should be saying that to you. Your fitness center and upcoming book release have created a buzz, Larry."

I let out an involuntary laugh. "It's been a long road to get here."

"I'm looking forward to reading the story," he said, pushing his ladder under the next fixture. "My wife's attending your book launch party." He paused and looked back at me. "Oh, did you speak to that lady looking for you?"

I shook my head. "Is she a member?"

He raised his hand to his chin. "No, but she knew you."

"Did she say anything else?"

"She left her business card for you."

"I'll look for it," I replied, curious to know who she was. "Thanks again."

I made my way into the office. Hastily, I rifled through the business cards on the desk but didn't recognize any of the names—more questions with no answers.

By 2:00, all the lights were up, and I craved fresh air. I followed the electricians into the bright sunshine and noticed a group of young members chatting on the bench. Amongst them was Ashley Grove. After snapping a selfie with her friends, she lurched to her feet.

"Oh hey, Larry!" she chirped, prancing over to me. "Erin and Savannah wanted a picture on your bench. Kinda cool, huh."

I hesitated to think of how many chapters I included, contemplating life while sitting on that bench. "Could that be because you sent them my manuscript?" I asked, slightly annoyed yet amused.

Ashley eyed me thoughtfully. "I know you're worried that no one in Melbourne Beach will have to buy the book, but just know they all joined The Gym because of it."

I nodded. There were no words. Or maybe there were too many racing around inside my head. After they strode by me, I sat on my suddenly infamous bench and answered Allison's call. She reminded me that we had her girls, Amelia, and Josie, over the weekend. We alternated weekends with her ex. She ended the call by telling me they would attend a birthday party after school. When I placed my phone on the bench, I noticed one of the club's most beloved instructors, Aurora Hermosa, heading my way.

"Hey, boss!" shouted the beautiful Brazilian brunette, "I have something for you."

She had her youngest son with her, and I gave him a high-five. "What's up, Zak?"

My eyes shifted to Aurora, who was fixated on a business card she pulled from her pocket.

"This lady came by to see you," she said. "It looks like she works for Captain Hook."

I blinked at the name Caroline Haines. Sales Director, RH Marketing Solutions. I sucked in a breath. "It's her."

"Who is she?"

I stared at her card. My whole body tingled with anxiety. "Caroline was a background character in *The Gym*. I only wrote her into the story because she seemed a hopeless romantic—"

"You dated her?"

"No, she was visiting her mother on vacation," I explained. "Anyway, she read my first novel while working out at The Gym. Caroline related to *The Show's* storyline, so we'd chat. I thought I'd gotten to know her. But…." I gripped her business card, collecting my scattered thoughts.

"But what?"

"Caroline Haines is now dating Stuart Grossman."

Aurora's eyes widened. "The tech tycoon?"

"Yes, which adds to an increasingly puzzling plot."

"Are you writing again?"

"I am…but I'm not sure how this could be titled *The Wedding*."

Aurora laughed and took her son's hand to head back into the parking lot. "Love conquers even the most puzzling plots." She paused, turning to me. "I know you'll figure it out, boss."

I smiled at her familiar vote of confidence. "Bye, guys."

I grabbed my phone. I took a moment to compose myself and then dialed Caroline's number. When I got her voicemail, I left her a message, hoping to catch up soon.

Thirty minutes later, The Gym was empty. We closed earlier on Fridays because the few members who came in after 3:00 agreed to be out by 7:00. Most Melbourne Beach residents looked to end the week with libations, not a workout. Typically, I'd be long gone by 2:00, but my employee, Sammie, was running late for her shift. I waited impatiently in the office as Ashley and her friends Snapchatted their exit.

The door beeped again.

"Ashley?" I called out, thinking they had left a phone on a treadmill.

"No, it's your star of chapter forty-two." I looked up and saw Caroline Haines standing at the check-in counter, holding two Starbucks coffees. She smiled grimly.

"Hi," I said, standing up shakily. "So, you got my voicemail."

She nodded once and handed me a Dark Roast. "The Gym looks great."

"Thanks."

Caroline didn't greet me with a hug. She entered the office and brushed past me in a Saint Laurent T-shirt and Tom Ford skinny jeans. I observed her curiously. Her head was on a swivel as she surveyed the room. After taking in all the pictures, I expected her to confess that she'd made a mistake and was dating a monster, but she was still under his spell. She put her purse and cup on the desk and pulled her phone from her pocket. The smell of coffee was in the air, mingled with traces of fine fragrance and a fabulous photo of Stuart.

What?

My eyes flickered at her screen. "This is my man," she boasted, quickly flipping to a photo with Captain Hook. "Stuart is Hook's business partner." Her head tilted to the side as she peered at me. "But you already know that, of course."

"Of course. Congratulations," I said. "I remember feeling like Dr. Phil when you sat in that same chair a couple of years ago."

"It's been twenty-seven months," she insisted. "It was three weeks before I met Stuart."

I nodded, thinking about what Tyler had said—about the real reason I was interviewed. "So, what brings you back to The Gym twenty-seven months later?" I asked, leaning back.

Caroline grinned at me. "You should be thanking me."

"Why is that?"

"I was the reason Carla interviewed you." She paused as I raised an eyebrow at her. "Wouldn't your curiosity get the best of you if you were the inspiration for a character in a book?" She glanced at a text, and I took a sip of coffee, wishing it was wine, waiting for her next move. "Since I work for Hook, and he owned the magazine, I convinced him to do the piece on you, so I could read it before it was released."

I played along. "How did you pull that off?"

"At the time, your…Cruella worked for the magazine. She was friends with Carla and knew she'd jump at the opportunity to interview you. So, when Hook told her I craved a sneak peek, she suggested your new novel for Carla's magazine piece."

I cleared my throat. "That interview was never published."

In the silence that followed, Caroline's eyes fell on her purse as she reached into it. "I want to show you something." She paused almost on cue. Being intelligent and thorough, she got right back to her agenda. "But first, I'm curious to know what else you've heard."

I sat up straighter. It was my turn to test her. "I heard your tech titan came up with this plan to interview me, so he could read a chapter he was paranoid about."

Caroline stared at me through narrowed, heavily made-up eyes. "Why would Stuart be paranoid about anything you wrote?"

"Tyler believes Stuart had something to do with Connor Lee's death."

Her eyes widened. "That's absurd. Hook no longer employs Tyler or Carla," she said shakily. "They're unstable. I'm scared to think what'll happen when Tyler finds out that Carla wrote a book detailing their volatile relationship while moving on to a doctor."

I found myself grinning and starting to frown at the same time. "I heard Carla wrote something else."

Caroline didn't answer me.

Instead, she pulled photo-copied pages of Carla's manuscript from her purse, and the conversation turned unexpected. "You and your Tinker Bell made Carla's book," Caroline said, handing me three pages. "Life can turn so quickly."

Without looking at her, I began reading.

Chapter Three — September 22, 2017.

The summer is over. Everything is different. I wish there were some "life" rewind button I could press. I liked it when Tyler would watch me lie on my bed, writing in my journal. It turned him on. He'd flip me over and kiss me. He'd always kiss me on the neck—in the same spot. Then he would push my legs apart, and his fingers were inside me. Those steamy nights were amazing—the sex, the conversations, and our long walks on the beach. It was enough to pretend that life had finally given us some feeling. Enough not to be numb. Enough to make his blue eyes tear up. "I'm going to make you a promise," he said. "I'm done with the partying. I want us to settle down. Get a place together. This has been the best summer of my life." That was true for both of us. Until he assumed I had something going with the bartender at the Yacht Club. He hated my flirting, and I feared his temper. So, it ended.

The rest of the page was blank.

Chapter Four — September 28, 2017.

I've been feeling depressed lately about a few things. I thought I was doing a good job hiding it, but certain colleagues have even noticed. I'm not ready to marry Tyler. Last night, he fucked me slowly, kissing me the whole time as I wondered how to end the relationship. He scares me. I'm tired of the bruises when he grabs me. It's his past. Witnessing his mother jump to her death would screw anyone up. I can't blame him. But that's not my concern, nor is his alcoholic brother, Sharky.

The rest of the second page was also blank, and chapter five was missing.

Chapter Six — September 30, 2017.

Stuart isn't helping my anxiety. He is charming and handsome. We were drinking at the same bars downtown when Tyler caught up. He followed me into the bathroom. "Take off your clothes," he said, locking the door. It was a command that infuriated me. And turned me on. His eyes moved over me as my bra hit the floor. We were so focused on connecting in this moment of rage that I couldn't recall how my panties ended up at my ankles. He spun me around, bent over the sink, and slowly entered me. After about a minute of him cupping my breasts and going at it, he pulled out, turned me back to him, stepped on my panties, raised my leg, and entered me again. "How's that?"

It's a rhetorical question, I assumed, because his kiss immediately followed, preventing me from answering. The next day, I knew Tyler wished that Stuart had never met Hook. Tyler's envious of The Monster. I had dreamt that Tyler bloodied Stuart's nose with a quick left on his new yacht. I visualized blood splattering all over the white upholstery. Maybe that was my subconscious screaming out. Perhaps I'd hoped they'd kill each other. I could start fresh.

I looked up from the page. My mind spun, processing this new information, or at least trying to. "This doesn't sound like the person who interviewed me," I said. "How fictionalized is this?"

"Larry, it's not. She's a scheming sex addict determined to ruin careers and lives. Carla Kimbrel is not to be trusted."

I recalled Carla saying that Caroline wasn't trusted, and I held up the pages. "Why are sections of this missing? I figured there would be more about her ex. Your beau, Stuart Grossman."

Caroline shrugged. "This is how they came. Here." She handed me another page. "Carla finished this after interviewing you. It turned out to be the last thing she wrote before being terminated from the magazine. I'll apologize in advance." Caroline paused, and as I gripped the pages, she added, "I'm sure your fiancée has some explanation for her actions."

Chapter Fifty — January 15, 2020.

Tyler called me today. I'm not sure why he called. He was pretty evasive. The last time I met him, we spoke about his depressed brother, Sharky—this time, I chose not to call him back. Maybe I'm scared about the future—this global conspiracy. Knowing what's about to happen has made me nervous. Perhaps it's complicating my feelings for Shawn. About our relationship. How could I not be? Stuart's assistant proved to me that Shawn still communicates with an ex. An ex who happens to be Peter Pan Man's muse. His Tinker Bell. Does Peter Pan Man's pixie dust wear off after a couple of years? He neglected to tell me that it does.

A little wave of anger passed over me. My gaze shifted to Caroline.

"Is Shawn a doctor?" I asked.

"Yes, Dr. Shawn Avery," she replied. "Did you know they still talk?"

I nodded and continued reading.

I only wish I knew Allison was talking to Shawn when I interviewed Larry for the upcoming release of his adventure in search of her love. I would have had one final question: So, Pan Man, does your soulmate call all her old boyfriends behind your back? Does Larry even care? I now believe it's all about book sales. That's the reason I pulled the piece on his novel. Fucking fairy tales don't exist, people! So, there you have it. More fucking irony. Life is full of it! Good night.

I folded the papers. I clenched my stomach, trying to keep my emotions under control while pondering my conversation with Tyler. Carla's rash decision to trash my interview now made sense: Deep down, she was a romantic hurt by past relationships. I handed the pages back to Caroline.

"How do you know the doctor?" I asked.

"I don't. A few of my colleagues are still friends with Carla on Facebook." Caroline lowered her voice. "My only intentions were to help you plug the release of *The Gym* while getting a sneak peek at what you wrote. But at least you now know it was Carla who screwed you. I'm sorry, Larry."

Somehow, I'd expected everything to make sense and that I'd know whom to trust. Instead, I sat there speechless with a growing sense that Allison hadn't even been truthful. She had recently denied knowing about Dr. Strange's invitation to meet her for a drink. When I told her his text flashed on her phone in front of me, she only casually explained that he wasn't serious.

My mind was racing.

All I had were more questions.

Then I heard Sammie's voice. "Larry, I'm sorry I'm late." I blinked at her. "Are you okay?"

"He needs a glass of wine," Caroline answered. She stood and gestured for me to go outside. "It was nice meeting you, Sammie."

I slowly stood up and followed Caroline. She suggested we finish the conversation at Sand on the Beach because she had read it was the restaurant where I'd met Sharky and Tyler. Being only a few miles up the road and on my way home, I agreed. I played it cool, but I was desperate to talk to Allison. I swallowed the lump in my throat, speeding away from The Gym when my call went to her voicemail.

A few minutes later, I gripped my wheel and spun into a spot. When I hopped out, Caroline zipped her new black BMW beside me. The power of the ocean stood her upright. "It's getting nasty out there!" Caroline shouted, slamming her car door. The rough surf reminded me of the night I met Sharky and Tyler. Despite the cool breeze, I was still hot and bothered.

After the server poured our wine, I leaned over my glass and began questioning Caroline. "Carla mentioned writing a piece about the election year. She uncovered something much darker."

Caroline's posture was straight and stiff. Her hands clasped together and fell to her lap. "No, it was fabricated nonsense," she said, shaking her head. "Worse than Tucker Carlson's conspiracy theories."

"I heard that piece cost Carla's boss her job."

"Oh, hell no," she scoffed. "She left the magazine because of personal problems."

I nodded hesitantly as another thought struck me. "Is it true that Stuart plans a presidential run in the 2024 election?"

Caroline smiled. "Yes. My handsome tech visionary is an ambitious, natural-born leader. Stuart has my vote and four years to solidify everyone else's."

"How do you feel about him being a Beijing booster?"

"Stuart's still selling me on China." She shrugged. "He says China's energy is great. He sees China as a great modern socialist country."

What?

I couldn't seem to move. To many Americans, this would be incomprehensible. I felt a chill from the inside out and forced a nod. "I realize you couldn't have known Stuart's brother, but I heard he felt differently about China. Have you ever questioned the boating accident?"

Caroline tucked her wind-blown hair behind her ear. "We should have sat inside." She gave me an odd look. "Anyway, it was a suicide. He was a depressed man—envious of Stuart."

"Why didn't they find his body?"

She appeared startled. "I have no idea." Her eyes drifted to the bar. "Excuse me. I need to make a call." When she walked away, Sammie texted me that she didn't get a good vibe from Caroline. Before I could respond, Caroline returned and handed her corporate card to the server. "Unfortunately, I must get going."

And so, with no further revelation forthcoming, I said, "I wrote you into *The Gym* because you seemed like a hopeless romantic searching for love." I paused and leaned over my wine glass. "Are you?"

Caroline sighed. "It's unrealistic to be hopeless to any emotion in my world." She raised her glass. "Cheers to the success of your new novel and the fitness center." We clinked glasses. "It should be an exceptional year. Once we get rid of Trump, we will celebrate again." She paused and looked at me. "You are a Democrat—right?"

"Business owners shouldn't talk about politics."

She stood up, answered a call, and turned back to me. "Goodbye, Larry."

I nodded. "Goodbye, Caroline."

•   •   •

Thirty minutes later, I was home. Strangely, the girls were there, but Allison was missing. Josie, her youngest, ran through the kitchen and mentioned that her mom was in her bedroom. I passed a bottle of wine on the family room coffee table and continued to the hallway that led to the bedrooms. Through Josie's closed door, I heard Allison on the phone. Somehow, I managed to knock softly.

"Allison?"

My fiancée stopped talking. And then said, "I'll be right there."

"I've been calling you."

"I'll be right there," she repeated.

A few minutes later, Josie approached me. "Is mom talking to a friend, Larry?" she said too inquisitively for a nine-year-old. I shifted my gaze to her, and she changed the subject. "So, what's for dinner?"

I sighed, wondering why they didn't eat at the party. "You didn't eat with your friends?"

"Oh, no," said Josie. "We didn't go to the party. We came straight home."

As I opened my mouth to question Josie, Allison spun into the family room, waving what looked like a poorly wrapped cigar. "Oh, it's nice for you to join us," I said, watching smoke trail her as she twirled to the French doors. "Is that cigar for me?" I watched her open the doors. "Or Dr. Strange?" I peeked outside, fearful he'd be standing there. "You didn't invite him over, did you?"

"Larry, stop. I'm smudging. It's sage. It cleanses a space and the people in it of negative energy."

I blinked at Allison and winked at Josie. "And taking calls behind locked doors: People are talking, darling."

Allison ignored me, moving into the living room as Josie smiled beside me. I could barely begin a conversation when a text flashed on my phone. I leaned over it on the coffee table and noticed it was Caroline. I suggested that Josie help her mother rid the house of demons so I could read the message: **I confirmed Carla's doctor boyfriend wants Allison back. I also heard you're writing again. If you choose to write this story, I must warn you that researching it will undoubtedly strain your relationship and ruin your happily ever after.**

Staring at her text, I couldn't help but wonder if she was right. So, I kept my eyes on the screen with my heart thundering and typed: **How do you know the doctor wants Allison back?**

I hit the arrow and impatiently stared at the dots as Caroline responded. Then, I read her reply: **Carla's still friends with someone at the firm. I'll get you proof.**

I swallowed hard.

It wasn't like I trusted Caroline, but I did trust Allison. I took a calming breath, not wanting to overreact, and walked outside to Google Dr. Shawn Avery. His impressive career flashed up with Instagram and Facebook pages, making this odd doc seem normal and single. There was something else, something I needed to check. I scrolled his Facebook page but found no proof that he'd begun dating Carla. In perpetual confusion, I searched Carla's name and realized she had no Facebook account.

I decided to let it go.

CHAPTER FIVE

PROOF CAUSES DOUBT

FEBRUARY 2, 2020

THE HOUSE

It was two days later, just before midnight.

My eyes flickered open to something I'd never expected to see: Caroline's proof. In short, Carla's old colleague, someone who reported to Caroline, sent her screenshots of Carla's texts detailing Dr. Shawn Avery's phone conversation with my fiancée.

In that call, Dr. Strange suggested that Allison stops teaching, which infuriated Carla.

Carla: Shawn let Allison vent about her lesson plans way longer than he listened to me bitch about anything.

Colleague: Maybe he felt bad for her.

Carla: Maybe he put the call on speaker because he wants her back.

Colleague: I doubt that it matters. I heard Allison's living out a fairy tale with the writer who owns The Gym.

Carla: You mean the salesman who's about to sell us a happily ever after?

Colleague: I think you're overreacting.

Carla: Overreacting? All men suck! Shawn ended the conversation by telling Allison she wouldn't have to work if she married him.

Only then did Caroline's warning have validity. Suddenly, I felt annoyed that things started to make sense.

Dr. Strange does want Allison back!

I eased myself out of our bed as a cool breeze rushed through the house. As I entered the kitchen, I caught sight of Allison through the open lanai doors. I stopped beside them, checking if my shadow could be seen, and listened. She was venting on her phone. Her issue was that we had been together too long without setting a wedding date. I would've let her pick the date if I hadn't refused to sell the house. But I had this notion that I could refinance the home, remove my ex from the mortgage, and then everyone would be happy. Unfortunately, these things took time, and I was focused on finishing my second novel. That didn't leave much time for her or our hopes and dreams.

What should I do?

Apologize, of course.

Then tell her everything I had heard.

I crouched down, out of her sight, returned to our bedroom, and jumped back under the covers, wide awake. I thought of all the magical moments that led me to Allison. In many ways, they almost seemed surreal.

I closed my eyes, battling a wave of skepticism. Aside from Dr. Strange, Allison had been talking to another ex-boyfriend. She insisted that these men were only friends, and I believed her. However, for the first time, I sensed that her need to be in contact with them had more to do with me. Perhaps I had taken her for granted. It's no secret that men and women are wired differently. But beyond the Mars and Venus thing, Allison had always yearned for attention. I regretted how long it took to write the story—the hours spent at my laptop, a grown man acting like a boy. 'Peter,' she'd say sarcastically, 'this adventure is taking too long to write!' I knew that rather cold, 'Peter, must you write on the weekends?' was wearing her out. But I didn't stop until the thoughts caught up to me: Unfortunately, sometimes, it was hours later. The next chapter always consumed me. I refused to have any interruptions. My writing was never anything I did to avoid her. I wrote because I loved storytelling. If I weren't obsessed with the process, I would've never finished either of my books. It wasn't easy to explain. And having all night to mull over how it affected my fiancée did not help the situation.

Her conversations with an old flame repeated relentlessly in my mind.

I flipped over my pillow, contemplating one that she had recently shared. Allison's ex had told her she deserved to be treated like a princess while insisting he'd sell his house to marry her. At the time, his direct dig only caused me to ask why she was even talking to him. Now I couldn't deny I was partially to blame. He showed up to appreciate what I didn't.

All it takes is a few words of appreciation and gratitude.

I released my breath in a slow sigh and dozed off, unsettled.

A few hours later, I walked out of our bedroom, surprised that Allison had started her day. "You're up early," I said as she closed her laptop and headed my way.

"Lesson plans," she moaned, passing me en route to the bathroom. "What's that look for?"

"I love you," I said, trailing behind her. "And I wanted to share some thoughts."

"Really?"

"Yes."

Allison glanced at me quickly, smiled—or winced. "Hold on, I have to pee," she replied, closing the bathroom door.

That's weird.

I waited, my breathing grew louder, and my pulse gained some speed. Then the toilet flushed, and the door opened. I took a shuddering breath. And blurted out: "Maybe I should sell the house."

She looked startled. "What happened to your spring refinancing plan?"

"It'll be more likely the summer. I have to pay off The Gym's new lights, fans, and treadmill."

Allison gave me a cold smile, seemingly taken aback. She reminded me that I assured her we'd be married when she turned forty-five. That was in October. Now, I only wished it wasn't February. With an obvious and overwhelming frown, she sat down by her laptop. "You're more concerned about the book launch than planning our wedding."

I glanced at the empty wine bottles on the coffee table and sighed heavily. "Why did you open another bottle last night?"

"Are you going to answer my question?"

"I'm not more concerned about my book launch. I only need more time if we refinance the house."

Her gaze drifted, thinking. "I love this house and neighborhood and our Fish House on the river." She paused, stood up, and smiled at me. "And I know you want to leave it to your kids. Lauren and Jerry would appreciate that." She shook her head. "I'm sorry. I guess I've had my family buzzing in my ear."

And Dr. Strange...and that old flame. There was so much that I wanted to say, but I kept my cool. "I understand. How's school going?"

She took a moment to compose herself. "I don't want to vent to you about that."

I took a slow breath and said dryly, "But you'll vent to whatshisname?"

To my surprise, she laughed. "Dr. Strange," she said, shaking her head. "Isn't that what you call him? If you can have an adult conversation without joking, we can talk about it—"

"I'm not joking."

She checked the time. "How about tonight at the Fish House?"

I couldn't endure an entire day without telling her what I'd heard. "There's something I've become aware of. Something about Dr. Strange—sorry, Dr. Avery."

Her arms crossed. "What is it?"

"He's dating Carla Kimbrel. She mentions you in her book."

Allison gave me a look that suggested she doubted it. "Why? What am I to her?"

"Someone too close to her, man," I replied. "And because of this, Carla pulled her piece on *The Gym*. She felt it overstated the magical appeal of our love story." I shook my head slowly. "And that's not fair…to us."

"Sounds like she has issues," Allison huffed, grabbing her phone. "Most women do."

Her comment left me momentarily speechless. Finally, as she scrolled through Dr. Strange's texts, I explained that Carla was a romantic who had a knee-jerk reaction after discovering another woman was talking to her boyfriend. My fiancée had no interest in hearing that and turned on the TV. "I wasn't aware Shawn was dating the woman who interviewed you. It can't be serious."

Her reaction made me feel worse. My mind went back to Caroline's warning. "Allison," I said, frowning, "This guy wants you back."

"We were never together. I went on a few dates with Shawn months before I met you, but I never considered him a boyfriend. I tried. I'm not attracted to him physically." Allison said this with perfect sincerity, and while reading a text, she added, "Have you heard of a company called EH Alliance?"

I watched her become impatient as she stared at his text. "No. What are you talking about?"

Allison's head moved: Her blue eyes stared into mine. "The virus I told you about."

My phone rang. It was Sammie at The Gym. I took a much-needed breath and answered, "Hey, Sammie—"

"Oh my God, Larry!" Sammie said frantically. "I had to walk outside to your bench."

I hit the speaker button and heard the panic in her heavy breathing. "What's wrong?"

"Nancy Neiman is stirring the pot again. She and the naggers want to cancel their memberships."

I gasped, "Just lower the air!"

"It's not that," Sammie whispered.

"Okay. Lower the music—"

"It's because of the Health Emergency."

"What?"

"Did you not hear?"

I spun to Allison, who was glued to a news report. "No."

"Larry, what should I say?"

"Hold on, Sammie—" I stepped closer to the TV as the World Health Organization spokesperson declared a Global Health Emergency. "What is this?" I muttered to Allison.

My fiancée slowly and deliberately turned to me. "It's the virus Shawn warned me about." She shot me a look and raised the volume. 'Human-to-human transmission has quickly spread and can now be found in the United States, Germany, Japan, Vietnam, and Taiwan,' the reporter stated, 'airport restrictions are imminent.' I almost dropped my phone as Sammie's voice startled me.

"Larry—what do you want me to do? The reports on the news are freaking them out."

I took her off speakerphone. "The media is the problem."

"Well, Nancy took our remote and turned all the TVs to CNN."

I checked the time. "Tell Nancy I'll call her at home—"

"At home?"

"Yes, get everyone to leave before Aurora's yoga class. And put ESPN on the TVs."

"Okay…okay, Larry. Hurry!"

"I'm on my way—"

Click.

CHAPTER SIX

FAKE NEWS

FEBRUARY 3, 2020

THE GYM

"Have things calmed down, Sammie?" I said, hurrying into The Gym's office. Only thirty minutes had passed since her frantic call, but the difference in Sammie was already apparent.

"Yes, Larry," she said, casually disinfecting our desk. "Nancy and the naggers are gone."

I surveyed the cardio area. "Has anyone else mentioned this Health Emergency?"

"Not since I changed the TVs to ESPN."

I opened my mouth and closed it again. I was determined to resist the urge to question this. Instead, I dropped my knapsack on an office chair and noticed Aurora leaning over the check-in counter. Discreetly, she asked if Caroline was a hopeless romantic or a villain. "The jury's still out," I said, thinking about Carla. "Didn't you say you knew the woman who interviewed me?"

She nodded. "Yeah. Carla dated my husband's best friend."

This girl gets around!

"Did he ever mention her?"

Aurora's voice was cautious. "Sure. He thought she was a romantic, looking to pen a love story based on her life." She grinned and whispered, "She's dated many men searching for the one. My husband felt she had an unrealistic expectation of his buddy. Why?"

I released a quick breath and shook my head. "Just piecing something together. Carla's research linked to this Health Emergency has me concerned."

Aurora gestured me to the yoga studio. "I'm not following?"

"It's crazy," I replied as we started walking. "I've questioned more than I ever had lately, and everything goes back to Carla's interview...." my voice trailed off.

"You've got a hot fitness center, a lovely fiancée, and a second novel coming out." She nudged me playfully. "How can life be any better?"

I shrugged. "I keep telling myself that, but that might be part of the problem."

"Nonsense," she chirped. "Back to your love story." She smiled. "I'd love to read about a summer wedding in book three."

I tried to smile. "So, have you heard about this Health Emergency?"

She turned the new lights on and gave me a quizzical glance. "No. Should we be boiling water?"

I hesitated. "No—no. It has to do with some mysterious virus."

She paused, pondering that. "Oh yes, my neighbors were talking about it. It's in China, right?"

"Yes—it began there," I sputtered, grabbing a paper towel. "But it's spreading."

"It's flu season. Big deal," Aurora replied as I wiped a handprint off the mirror.

"Well, Allison...and others know an infectious disease doctor who believes it will be a problem. The news is reporting it as a Global Health Emergency."

Aurora pulled her long dark hair off her flawless face and put it in a ponytail. "It's an election year. Don't let the media scare you. Some of them would love to slow the economy to smear our President. Things are good and are only going to get better." She raised her voice. "FOUR MORE YEARS!"

I winced when my phone pinged.

I noticed it was Tyler and read his text: The mainstream media only tells one side of this story. Carla has proof that Australia's public broadcaster, the ABC, is relentlessly repeating whatever propaganda China releases. Their reporting is changing how people think. They believe the fake news. And even worse, anyone suggesting this virus leaked from a lab is labeled a crazy conspiracy theorist.

How does that happen? I replied. If this virus was leaked, why aren't more scientists coming forward?

Tyler's response flashed faster than I anticipated: They fear losing future research funding or having their experiments barred if the world finds out this virus came from a lab engaging in biological warfare.

I swallowed hard as members filed into the studio for Aurora's yoga class. I forced a smile, greeted them, and turned to Aurora as she approached me with a look of concern. She motioned me through the door. "Who texted you?" she asked quietly. "You don't hide your emotions well."

I meandered over to a spin bike and faced her. "Tyler Harrison."

"Sharky's brother?" she asked curiously.

I nodded. "Lately, Tyler's had me second-guessing things."

She shook her head. "What could you be second-guessing? You're living out a fairy tale."

After a slight pause, I answered, "A darker version of it."

"What does that mean?"

Tyler's text rattled me, so I exclaimed, "A planned pandemic!"

Aurora laughed awkwardly. "What's gotten into you?"

I sighed. "Again, I'm not sure. I've spent a ton of money and question if the timing was right."

She reassured me that the fitness center was doing well and wondered why I was acting strangely. Since I refused to sound certifiable, I only told her that a summer wedding sounded great. Aurora ate that up. "YES!" she shouted. "This makes me so happy."

I shuddered at the thought. A fall wedding would be questionable at this point. I tried to backtrack but only babbled about the refinancing plan to get my ex-wife off the mortgage. Aurora always enjoyed the imaginary backdrop of my stories. With a girlish grin, she insisted that my Tinker Bell loved me and would wait amidst a flurry of pixie dust.

Before I could explain my emotions, a member interrupted us. "Class should've begun, guys."

I lowered my voice. "I'll talk to you later, Aurora."

Aurora smiled at me. "Stop worrying, boss," she pleaded. "This is going to be our best snowbird season yet!"

I blinked at another text. Again, it was Tyler: **On a separate note, I had heard you collect sports memorabilia. I have a couple of jerseys from your generation. I'll give you a good deal on a signed Reggie Jackson and Gretzky Jersey. Let me know. I'm desperate for money.**

I didn't respond.

I walked away, annoyed. And the annoyance stayed with me for the rest of the day.

Tired and frustrated, I entered the house around 6:00.

Allison was curled on the couch, reading an email on her laptop, as a CNN news bulletin scrolled across the TV. Without a hello, she picked up her wine glass. "I have to respond to this," she said. "It's from the girl's father. Oh, and Shawn's no longer with Carla." Allison took a sip, turned up the volume, and added, "This is the latest update on the Health Emergency."

I stepped into the family room, trying to process what was happening, and turned to the TV. 'The CDC confirmed the first U.S. case in Washington state on January 18,' stated the reporter. 'The White House assembled a Task Force to coordinate efforts to prevent, contain, and mitigate the spread of this deadly disease.'

I grabbed a nearly empty wine bottle off the coffee table, exhausted. Without looking up, Allison urged me to open another bottle. I gathered my frantic thoughts. "You finished this one fast."

"I have a ton going on right now, Larry."

"Can we talk about it?" I asked.

Her fingers typed furiously. "What?"

I sighed dramatically. "We used to enjoy a bottle of wine together catching up…."

"Wait…shit," she said, glancing at a text that flashed on her phone. "Hold on. It's Amelia." She responded to the message and added, "I have to rewrite this part of the email." Allison placed her phone down and began typing. "What's wrong?"

"Oh, I don't know…I'm just wondering why I haven't held your precious head in my hands, stared into your beautiful blue eyes, and kissed you lately?"

Her eyes narrowed angrily at her laptop. "Maybe because Carla's dark fairy tale has consumed you."

I shook my head. "Allison, everything feels different. I used to come home to kisses and laughter…." my voice trailed off.

Allison didn't answer right away. When she finally did, it was about her ex. "I can't believe this ass is blaming me for everything."

I couldn't recall her nervously biting down on her lip as she had been. With an eye on the news, my thoughts went back to her statement about Dr. Strange. Then I said, "Why are you two speaking every night?"

She looked up at me. "He's the father of my children."

"Not him. Dr. Strange."

She gestured to the CNN report and reminded me that the doctor had warned her about the virus. I reiterated that Carla did the same, but my fiancée only believed CNN. Without mentioning Dr. Strange, she insisted the virus was deadly.

I remained motionless, gripping the wine bottle, reciting Aurora's line: "It's a virus during flu season. So, relax."

"If you don't open more wine, I want the rest."

I brought the bottle to my lips, tilted my head back, and finished it. "There's none left."

Allison's gaze shifted back to her laptop, riled. She leaned forward, muttering obscenities at her ex-husband's reply. "I have to call my attorney," she said, glaring at me. She started to get that sorry-for-herself feeling. "Nothing feels right anymore, Larry," she added, shaking her head. "Why does everything feel so different?"

I sighed again. "I just said that."

"Said what?" she said distractedly. "I'm asking why everything feels so different."

"Could it be that the news is disturbing, this emailing of your ex is obsessive, and our wine times have officially gotten out of hand?"

"You never said that to the leading lady of your first novel."

"Allison, *The Show* was ten years ago. I can't drink as we did in *The Gym* anymore."

She shook her head. "Oh, the storyline that had you opening wine in my apartment before breakfast?"

"It was 11:30, and I was fifty," I pouted, sounding like a child convincing a parent why it's okay not to eat vegetables. "Not fifty-three—" Ashley's text cut me off: **My depressed mother is drunk again. This Health Emergency is freaking her out. Can you talk?**

I replied: **I can't, I'm fighting with my Tink.**

Ashley messaged: UGH! I hate it when there's trouble in Never Land!

My Tink's eyes slid to her empty wine glass. "I need more wine tonight," she pleaded. "I'll only have one glass tomorrow. Okay?"

My heart felt like it sank into my chest. "Fine," I said quietly but was unable to move.

Allison gazed up at me, her blue eyes steeped in sorrow. "Thanks."

My arms crossed, recalling our New Year's resolution to cut back on the wine. I wanted to remind Allison of the two blissful nights we didn't drink, went to bed early, made love, and fell asleep in each other's arms, happy and healthy. I looked at her, and in the depths of her eyes, I saw the pain she had only mentioned. I thought it best to tell her how sorry I was that I had taken her for granted lately, but I flinched when she yelled, "I can't believe I married this man!"

This is ridiculous.

"Allison, you have an IQ of a hundred and forty," I exclaimed. "How can you get so worked up by these emails?"

Her eyes closed briefly, and when she opened them again, she was no longer looking at her laptop. She was looking straight at me. "Larry, please open more wine."

I stared at her, speechless.

She tried to smile at me. "You should eat dinner, too."

"I've lost my appetite."

"Oh, well, I like the Joel Gott."

I muttered, "I've seen the recycle bin."

Allison's mouth puckered with disapproval, but she didn't say anything. I staggered to the wine rack, opened a Joel Gott cabernet, took a long sip, and left the rest beside her. I kissed her cheek as her bloodshot eyes narrowed at another email and headed to bed, listening to her curse her ex.

•　　•　　•

Two hours later, Allison barged into the bedroom, ranting about having to do all the chores around the house. I sat up, panicked, and assured her I would help. But that only made her enraged.

"I'm cleaning now," she growled, tipsy. "You should want to clean with me."

I blinked at her in disbelief. "Allison, I never want to clean. Why do you think I want to clean when I'm starving and half asleep?"

"Why are you looking at me weird?"

WHAT?

I flipped my pillow over and pounded it with my fist. "I get home, exhausted; you don't say hello, but you're cursing your laptop, hysterical over this Health Emergency, and insisting on more wine."

She swayed in place for a moment. "You have a bad temper, little boy. I hope you know that."

Breathe.

"Okay, Allison." My voice was quiet, barely a whisper. "Please come to bed."

"No!" She slammed her hands on her hips. "You drive me crazy."

I collapsed on the pillow. "Waking me up at midnight to clean the house will keep me sane."

"Keep it up, and I'll vacuum the bedroom. It would be senseless to sleep over a dusty floor."

I mumbled, "Who's sleeping?"

"What did you say?"

"I said life would be senseless without music, so blast the Bose while you're at it."

She stormed out. "I might. I do everything, and it's too much!"

"Say hi to Dr. Strange for me."

CHAPTER SEVEN

WHAT WASN'T SAID

FEBRUARY 4, 2020

THE HOUSE

I paced the hallway the next night, rereading Allison's loving and remorseful morning texts. My first emotion was pure elation, but panic pierced through the joy as I recalled the nights before. I could no longer deny those texts came after evenings of instability.

Still, I found ways to differentiate Allison from Ashley's mother, who had used alcohol to mask her feelings of depression.

Even though our wine times had turned into scenes reminiscent of the cult classic *Sideways*, I blamed the sorrowful script replaying in my mind on Carla's dark fairy tale.

Maybe I can't stomach a real mess of corruption.

Maybe I don't want to be shown the makings of her dark fairy tale.

I wish I'd never met Carla!

I sighed, quite rattled.

But why am I so fascinated by her?

I wandered into the living room, forcing my thoughts forward only to look behind us at our past. My gaze landed on one of my favorite photographs of Allison from our second date. I lingered by our picture wall, craving the days gone by: Two years of magical memories seemed like a lifetime ago.

I checked the time.

It was 10:18.

The house was finally quiet.

At 10:30, I took a breath and held it when Allison came out of Josie's room. She looked defeated, as if she'd lost a fight. I glanced at our open wine bottle, hoping her argument with her younger daughter wouldn't trigger her to finish it. I hugged her tight after she approached me, but it didn't help. She knew I had been waiting to talk and only took a second to reassure me that she'd be back in a few minutes.

I nodded as she hurried into our bedroom and decided it was best not to say anything. Rather than making things worse, I headed to my notepad on the kitchen table. I wrote in times of turmoil and sat down, intrigued by an article I had found in a local newspaper.

After a few minutes, I started reading my notes:

'The Chinese government views Stuart Grossman as a vital business partner. Grossman has brought the children of Beijing's party bosses into his companies. He has partnered with new firms to expand his reach while manipulating many. I left in 2017, shortly after Grossman partnered with James Hook at my old firm in Melbourne, Florida. I was able to retire comfortably, but I fear for those who must learn to live a lie,' David Ford, CEO (2004-2017), stated on 2/4/2020.

I shook my head: I was angry and frustrated. Then, I picked up my pen and wrote:

A month ago, I asked myself how my life could get any better. Today I'm asking myself how it can get any worse.

I laughed at the absurdity of it all and continued writing after Allison rushed back into Josie's room. These weren't notes: I was writing as if this was a chapter to be included in a book. I didn't question it. I continued writing:

Shortly after my fiancée returned from our bedroom, she sat beside me, knowing we had to talk.

WE HAD TO TALK!

I smiled at her.

She took a deep breath, as if she didn't want to have the conversation, but exhaled and began. "I miss how things were," she said, glancing back at a CNN report. "This virus is spreading."

I nodded. "We should turn off the news and make time for ourselves."

Allison continued. "I know you're writing again. I can't stand reading your notes about Carla's dark fairy tale." She paused and sighed. "I can't deal with losing you right now...especially to anything Carla is a part of."

"Again, Carla's saying the same thing as Dr. Strange."

"I don't care!" she snapped. "You're writing again."

I swallowed hard. "I don't know what I'm writing, so don't worry. I am focused on us."

"Well, I'm worried about us. And not just us as a couple. This Health Emergency is scary—" A loud crash interrupted us.

We hurried to Josie's bedroom, but I was trailing Allison, and the door abruptly shut in my face. "No worries, my nose isn't broken."

I took a couple of steps back.

Tensions were high.

Voices were raised.

Then I asked, "Is everything okay?"

Tears were shed.

I waited.

A few minutes passed.

Maybe ten.

Then, Allison came back out. Her eyes widened, and she was thoroughly stressed out. "I have to take care of something," she said, grabbing her laptop. "Josie needs her mom tonight. I'll explain tomorrow."

I sat alone, impressed by Allison's motherly love, yet still contemplating what wasn't said.

CHAPTER EIGHT

THE SHOW THAT NEVER ENDS

FEBRUARY 5, 2020

THE HOUSE

Morning came too fast.

Allison sat cross-legged on the family room couch, reading my first novel. I poured a cup of coffee and offered her a refill. She shook her head in silence and turned a page. I asked her if she wanted a bagel with schmear, and I smiled. Her weary blue eyes rolled.

A silence fell between us.

I wanted to move toward my fiancée but remained still. I had wrestled through another long and sleepless night. I craved caffeine trying to decipher what was happening: Insomnia made it a laborious undertaking. I stood there for several minutes, completely lost. I couldn't believe she was rereading *The Show* now. We needed to talk about our relationship, and I certainly wasn't interested in explaining an emotional affair with that story's leading lady.

However, at this point, I would welcome a conversation about Wendy Darlington if it meant avoiding another argument about Carla Kimbrel.

At least, I thought so until Allison closed my novel and said, "Explain this weird cheek fetish you had with Wendy?"

My mouth fell open a little. "Wendy, who?"

"Cut the shit."

"It wasn't a fetish….and for the record, your cheeks are better than hers."

"Shut up, Larry," Allison said, her eyes crinkled in concern. "What would happen to us if The Gym closed?"

I wasn't sure how I ended up on the couch across from her, but there I was. "I should explain the cheek fetish," I said, backtracking. "You deserve an explanation."

"I'm serious. What would you do if it closed?"

I cleared my throat. "Allison, you know our love has magically transformative powers, which gave us a new understanding of life," I said, shifting uneasily. "We live a life that matters. Us. Together. Regardless of what I do: A life of love."

Allison insisted that she was raised differently. I shook my head and gathered my thoughts. I wanted to respond, but my mouth was dry. I could tell by her expression that she was talking to her father again. She wore the same all-knowing look every time she did. They shared this love-hate relationship, and when they were good, my fiancée would buy into his outdated opinions. Finally, she confirmed my thoughts. "My father doesn't believe in fairy tales." Her tone was matter-of-fact. "He believes the man should be the provider. He felt I could stop teaching soon, but this Health Emergency has changed everything."

"I definitely need more coffee."

"Larry, you will not be able to provide if The Gym is closed."

"Allison, most households need two incomes. Tell your father it's not 1965," I whined, spilling my coffee. "Shit."

Allison placed my novel on the coffee table and sat beside me, feeling far away. "Everything you laughed about seems to be returning to haunt you…us," she said quietly. My heart beat faster. She continued, "You wrote a book that ended a well-paying career and burned every bridge back to that industry. It's irresponsible."

"Is this leading to a question?"

She nodded. "Can you reinvent yourself yet again?"

"Yes. I've done it before, and if necessary, I'll do it again."

"Your ego will be your demise."

What?

Now it's evident that she'd been up late texting again. I took a slow breath to calm down. Then, slowly, I growled, "I see Dr. Strange still has you on edge."

"Larry, Shawn knew this virus would change our lives, and I can't turn on the news without my depression overwhelming me."

I closed my eyes for a moment. When I reopened them, Allison looked at me with quiet desperation. I recognized that look and flinched, unable to help it. "We shouldn't be watching the news."

"It's not just the Health Emergency," she said frustratedly. "I'm tired of walking on eggshells around you."

I jerked back angrily. "Well, I'm tired of buying three bottles of wine every night."

"Well, I'm sick of the five-star reviews on a book that details the demise of your lucrative career."

My head slumped forward. "We're back to the book?"

She ignored me. "A book about a talented man who recklessly threw it all away." She paused, took a breath, and lowered her voice. "But I'm better acquainted with the other guy. The man who can look directly into a woman's soul and make them believe in every fairy tale they've ever been told. I want to be the woman who gets to enjoy that man. The man I know you are."

I felt like she was pushing me away to pull me back in. I shrugged confusedly. "So, do you agree with your father or me?"

Allison rolled her eyes at my sarcastic tone. "You," she said. "But I'm confused and worried about our future. Everything feels different." She paused and crossed her arms over her chest in a defensive posture. "And don't bring up the wine. Alcohol is not the center of the conflict."

"Well, it sure as hell seems like it is."

"You drink a lot, too, Larry."

I nodded. "We are drinking too much. And I'll go one step further; I'm a complicated, flawed individual!" I snapped. "But I can stop drinking whenever I want. I've proved that. Can you?"

"You can be so mean."

"I'm not trying to be mean, Allison."

"It comes naturally to you, Larry. Shawn was right."

"Excuse me?"

"You have no compassion for anyone who isn't perfect."

I took a breath and exhaled. "I'm far from perfect."

"Yes, but everybody is fond of your flawed character. You sold that shit perfectly, and your readers love you!"

I wanted Allison to stop talking because everything she said caused me more pain. There were things I needed to say. However, my jaw tightened. Then it just came out, "Think happy thoughts, please."

Her gaze was steady on *The Show*. "I'm not interested in your Never Land humor."

I resisted the urge to say anything else that would be spiteful. "I felt we needed to lighten the mood. Please smile. I adore your smile."

She pushed my novel to the edge of the coffee table and plowed on. "How could you do what you did with Wendy, not realizing it wouldn't blow up?"

I pinched the bridge of my nose, and as calmly as possible, I reminded her that it wasn't sexual—I thought I had control. Allison slowly turned her head to me. Her blue eyes were watery. She questioned how I felt now, ten years later. I swallowed hard. "I lost Wendy, someone I wasn't prepared to lose—that hurt. But there hasn't been a day that I didn't remember what I'd thrown away and how I affected the mother of my children. I have regrets about how I handled everything." I paused, shaking my head, and quietly added, "I spent years trying to save my marriage. That didn't make it into any book because no one wants to read about that." I was irritable; I took a slow breath to finish my thought. "Now, I'm grateful to be starting over with you."

She sighed. "Well, I am too," she responded, shifting her gaze to the news. She frowned, turned it off, and added, "But I can't see you interviewing for any position in your old industry because your book is *The Show* that never ends."

"The Gym is not going to close."

"If it does, everyone thinks you are screwed."

"You mean the men who trash me because they want you back?"

Allison's eyes were apologetic and full of regret. "Lately, I've wished you treated me like they do."

My stomach clenched. "Your morning texts starkly contrast your evening instability, proving you're apologizing for your actions."

"You make me feel like I need to apologize for being sad."

"Allison, I love you. In two years, I've never seen you like this."

"I knew you couldn't handle me," she said, standing up. "Shawn knew it too. He listed many things about me that you can't handle."

More of Dr. Strange's greatest hits.

I glared at her, and as she turned away, I refused to lose my composure. "Dr. Strange doesn't know me, and I'm not interested in what he says about you."

The pain in her eyes was evident again as she only looked to change the subject. "You need to get the passes to Ashley for her friends to attend Aurora's yoga class."

I checked the time. "Shit…."

"I'm surprised your little friend hasn't texted you."

I glanced at my phone, spooked by Ashley's missed message: HELLO! WHERE ARE YOU?

I tucked my phone in my back pocket as Allison drove her point home while leaving my concern in her rearview mirror. "No one's taking those classes during this Health Emergency, so hurry."

I couldn't leave her like this. I took a breath and forced myself to stay positive. "I'd like to take you to dinner tonight," I said. I tried to sound upbeat, but she could tell I was exhausted.

She tilted her head, pushing her lips into a frown. "No, we should start watching our money."

I shook my head. "I refuse to allow this Health Emergency to ruin us, Allison."

Tiredly, I pushed myself off the couch. I waited, and the silence stretched between us. Then, slowly, I turned and walked out.

•   •   •

For the next three days, we stopped watching the news. Things were better, but still quite different from the way things were. Our drinking dictated our nights. My temper would flare as her mood swings worsened. It became increasingly tiresome to look into her bloodshot eyes and see someone else lash out with words they'd never say sober. Allison's depression had darkened her beautiful soul. Knowing I'd endured too much of her evening instability, she continued to wake up remorseful, hug me, and tell me I must genuinely love her. And I did.

That said, I couldn't deny we had entered a time that only Carla could explain. Although I was fascinated by her dark fairy tale, I was in complete denial that it could become our reality.

Exhausted, I'd go to bed early, pretending this Health Emergency would miraculously end.

CHAPTER NINE

SHOCK, ANGER, AND DENIAL

FEBRUARY 11, 2020

THE GYM

It was a chilly Monday three days later.

Ashley texted me after dinner, insisting we speak before Tuesday's yoga class. Since Allison was waiting for me to start our movie, I hastily agreed, silenced my phone, and returned my attention to my fiancée. Although we never talked about everything pulling us apart, we were content not to have another argument where every word felt like a blow to our hearts. This avoidance of reality allowed us to have some fun again. And that was a start.

We finished our wine, didn't open another bottle and got cozy on the family room couch. As the movie began, I rubbed Allison's feet, energized by her warm smile. It was an enjoyable evening, reminiscent of how things were before Carla's dark fairy tale had cast an ominous shadow into our lives.

At 5:48 a.m., I traded my coffee for my keys and headed to meet Ashley.

Just before daybreak, I pulled into The Gym's parking lot. As I walked into the office, the early morning regulars were uncharacteristically quiet, watching the latest Health Emergency update. Simply thinking about this virus made my throat dry. I took a sip of water and began disinfecting the treadmills with an eye on the door, anxiously awaiting Ashley's arrival.

Soon after I finished the last treadmill, a member questioned a tapping sound on the back door. Immediately, I envisioned my young beta reader in a hoodie attempting some secret knock that I forgot about and rushed to retrieve the key in a cabinet under the desk. I grabbed it and banged my head when her elbows crashed on the check-in counter with a thud.

"Walk outside to your bench," Ashley said and forced a smile.

I rubbed my head. "Were you at the back door?"

She lowered her voice. "We can't talk here."

I smiled awkwardly at the members gawking at us and followed Ashley outside. "That was discreet," I said, eyeing her curiously. "What's up?"

Her brown eyes widened. "Really?"

"Yes, what's wrong?"

Ashley's expression flashed from excited to something darker. "Do you remember my psychic reading?"

I nodded hesitantly. "Yes."

In rapidly broken phrases, Ashley reiterated that the tarot card reader predicted how 2020 would end an innocent time. She reminded me that I wrote this story full of corruption, conflict, and chaos in her dream. Ashley paused to let that sink in but was further unsettled by what must have been my skeptical look. She turned to watch the sunrise. "I can't believe this is going to happen, Larry," she said slowly. "I'm scared. For everyone."

I took a few steps forward and placed a reassuring hand on her shoulder. "Ashley, those card readings are meant to entertain more than actually to predict anything."

She jerked her head to me. "Tyler Harrison put me in touch with Carla Kimbrel to get my feedback on her new manuscript. It's the story the psychic predicted. Aren't you watching the news?"

I pulled away from her and shrugged. "No. We've been watching movies instead of the news. Things have been better—" she interrupted me.

"Well, the real world isn't Never Land, Peter! Everything is only getting worse. Tyler told me he's been texting you relentlessly, but you refuse to believe any of this."

I drew in a sharp breath. "I know there's a serious virus out there."

"A serious virus?" she shouted. "Carla's book ends in the future when imagining the unthinkable is no longer a stretch: A two-year global pandemic that changes everything. Have you read this?"

I cocked an eyebrow. "No, but a global pandemic will not engulf the world." I paused, fidgety with irritation, and then added, "I'm not denying this virus might've been leaked from a lab—" Ashley shut me up with just a look and handed me her phone.

"Carla uncovered a global conspiracy," she said, gesturing to the manuscript. As I glanced at the title of the chapter: A Dystopian Nightmare, she added, "Read this page."

We exchanged a look.

Then, I began reading:

'I recalled our article: Big Business Backs Big Government to Gain Control of Everything, Including the White House! I knew the world would drastically change when we finished that piece. It's as if we've lived out the most twisted dystopian novel ever written. It's now 2023, crime and inflation are out of control, and the mainstream media still swears this engineered virus came from a wet market. Generations from now, they will look at this moment in time and wonder how it happened—but wait. That brings me to my history lesson. The Revolutionary War, the Civil War, World War II, and The Pandemic are each eighty years apart for a reason. Eighty years is the lifespan of a human being and, therefore, the limit of personal memory and experience. New generations will refuse to accept the compromises and deceptions of the past. Thus, repeating history. I often think about Dr. Shawn Avery, a history buff who knew the magnitude of corruption surrounding this virus cover-up. He had been ridiculed since December 2019, when he first warned me of this nightmare. I only wish he wasn't naïve about the corruption inside the bureau. He shunned the warnings and refused to believe the FBI would read my notes on this story, raid a journalist's home, and murder the whistleblower who was ready to expose the virus's origins—'

Ashley grabbed her phone. "Larry, say something."

"Did you want me to read this or not?"

She continued, "Carla's interviewing scientists who know. Her book has been extremely accurate to this point." Ashley scrolled to a chapter that takes place in the future. "Read about the Big Pharma lobbyists and the vaccines." I blinked desperately, trying to keep up. "Carla linked this virus to a planned vaccine rollout, government regulations, mandates, enormous transfers of wealth, and the President's demise."

"I don't see Trump approving any government mandates."

"That's her point. In her book, the President doesn't. And because of it, he plays right into the hands of the media. Trump tweets enraged outbursts as they push this fear factor narrative by using supposed experts who claim to have scientific data that is more scripted than researched. The White House is held solely responsible for mishandling a Health Emergency that escalates into a global pandemic. Small businesses like your beloved gym don't stand a chance. Ask yourself why the WHO advised against any travel restrictions to China while being aware of this virus."

My heart was beating considerably faster than I wanted to admit. I thought about Stuart Grossman's massive donations to the WHO and wondered if he made these contributions to control them. "Does Carla mention her ex making any donations to the WHO?"

"Yes," Ashley said. "Toxic politics fuel this virus. Many honest doctors and journalists were silenced." She paused, took a breath, and added, "Do you recall Caroline Haines working for Big Pharma?"

My head wobbled a nod. "Yes."

"Stuart Grossman has used Caroline for her Big Pharma connections. Global elites, Big Pharma, and Dr. Frank Folie are players in this horror story. One man dies, and another man gets rich. Carla referenced the Spanish Flu of 1918. Think Vicks vapor rub and Lysol."

"Hold on. I've heard Folie's name before. Who is he?"

"Folie is America's highest-paid career bureaucrat. He directed the health agency to approve millions of dollars of federal funding for experiments on bat coronaviruses that occurred at the Wuhan Institute. Folie knew that gain-of-function research with bat coronavirus experiments was being conducted to infect human cells. Carla refers to Folie as a liberal icon who, along with China, denies any knowledge of gain-of-function research. At the same time, hospitals are granted money for deaths related to the virus. This, in turn, gives the media more deaths to report while instilling so much fear that they control a dangerous narrative through their far-reaching news outlets. And get this, Folie's wife is head of an organization that approves drugs for the FDA." Ashley paused, crossed her arms, and added, "I can go on and on, but I came to talk to you about something else in Carla's story."

My mind was racing with all kinds of things, but nothing I wanted to say out loud. For starters, Stuart Grossman was an American Marxist who shared Folie's political views, and his brother was mysteriously killed, and this virus was spreading. Then I caught Ashley's stare and anxiously asked, "What is it?"

"Carla dated Dr. Avery."

My stomach dropped. "I know. Tyler and Caroline briefed me."

She gave me a solemn nod. "Did you know Dr. Avery talks to Allison and wants her back?"

"She never considered him to be a boyfriend."

"Larry, this has been a weird year already: That might've changed."

My voice trembled. "It hasn't." I tried to explain, but I couldn't. Everything that Allison and I had been avoiding walloped me there at that moment. I swallowed heavily, only wanting to call my fiancée. Then Ashley patted my arm.

"Are you okay?"

"I don't know."

"I know you love each other; I do. But Carla has eavesdropped on Allison's conversations with this doctor. She believes you've changed since finishing your book. Your fiancée is starting to doubt you can deal with her depression. The doctor suffers from depression as well. They have that in common."

"Get to your point, please."

"The doctor has convinced Allison that The Gym will close because of this global pandemic."

"There's a virus out there," I yelled frustratedly. "It will not turn into a global pandemic."

Ashley said, "Well, Carla's book has been right about everything else."

I thought about Allison's recent concerns about The Gym and sighed angrily. "Carla has fictionalized much for her novel," I insisted, still trying to push it all out of my mind. "Her overdramatization of Allison's friendship with this guy has book sales written all over it."

"In her book, Italy locks down around this time."

My mind was paralyzed now. "What?"

Ashley handed me her phone again. "Carla figured a mandated lockdown would be in place by next week."

I stood in a state of shock. "I supposed her research would produce certain coincidences, but the White House will not implement a lockdown. The Chinese Communist Party does not rule us."

Ashley thought for a second and shook her head. "Listen, Aurora told me you've been concerned about this. I would choose to play it off too. Just promise me you'll read it," she said quietly, hugging me. "I would hate to see your fairy tale come out with your business devastated and your Tinker Bell in someone else's arms."

CHAPTER TEN

HER "I LOVE YOU MORE!" NEVER CAME

FEBRUARY 24, 2020

THE GYM

Ashley raced into the yoga studio like clockwork.

She held up her phone. "Italy's been locked down!"

I continued sweeping the studio as she circled me with a CNN YouTube video. The reporter said, 'The Italian government issued Decree-Law No. 6 of February 23, 2020, containing urgent measures to manage the Epidemiological Emergency, effectively locking down the country—' I held up a hand for silence.

"Ashley, I know," I muttered. "I'm having difficulty breathing right now, so please stop."

Her brown eyes widened with an uncontrollable urge to continue. "I heard your trainers took a leave from The Gym, and you're canceling next month's fitness classes."

I glanced over my shoulder. "Yes. Members have been frantic about it all morning—" Their angry voices interrupted me.

My chest tightened.

We walked out of the studio as members echoed CNN's sentiment to lockdown the country.

"Trump better act now!" a voice hollered.

"Italy is piling dead bodies in trucks," another added. "That idiot keeps talking about conspiracy theories when he should put a stay-at-home order in place."

Then, Nancy Neiman made eye contact with me.

Fuck!

"Larry!" she snapped. "What you're doing about this?"

I felt lightheaded. "We're disinfecting the equipment while we monitor the latest developments. Please wash your hands frequently," I said, turning away from them when the office line rang. "Excuse me."

Ashley followed, mumbling obscenities before glancing at the ringing phone. "Are you going to answer that?"

"Can you?" I replied, grabbing my Evian. I took a much-needed gulp and poured the rest over my head.

A minute later, Ashley ended the call with a raised eyebrow at me and held up another member's name, who froze their account for March. She pulled her dark hair back, squinted at me, and said, "Did your office shower help?"

I smiled faintly and noticed Allison was calling. I wiped my wet face with a gym towel and answered, somewhat flustered. "Hey."

"Hey, I wanted to apologize. I was overly sensitive last night and a bit irrational."

Taken aback, I checked my phone screen, confirmed it was my fiancée, and said, "Well, I'm sorry for being short with you."

"Guess what?"

"What?"

She chirped, "I've been smelling your pillow!"

I straightened, turning back to Ashley. She pretended not to hear. Then I muttered, "Good." I grinned. "It's been a while since you had."

Allison laughed. "I know. Do you remember the day I took it to school with me—well, I left it in the car—but…."

I cleared my throat. "Sure do."

"Is Ashley eavesdropping again?"

"She sure is, but go on."

"Anyway, I'd love to spend some quality time together tonight. How about dinner and another movie?"

Shit!

I took a slow breath and said, "That sounds great, but tonight I have a cleaning crew coming in to disinfect everything after we close."

"No!" Anxiety crept into her voice. "Nothing's right anymore. Everything feels bad."

"Try to be open to the bad stuff leading to better things."

"I don't know if I can."

I swayed, pressing the phone against my wet ear, wishing I hadn't dumped the Evian over my head, and quietly said, "Things have been better between us: Focus on that."

"Larry, that's only true because we watch movies as the real world darkens."

I tilted my head in frustration. "Allison, we don't know what will happen, but I'm here for you. We have each other. We can get through anything, so please call me if you need to vent." As she spoke about her day, I couldn't deny that her worsening depression and sudden mood swings were wearing me out. When I reminded her that alcohol was a depressant, she looked to end the call. I suggested we plan something for the weekend, but she only responded that we had the girls and shouldn't be spending frivolously. I sighed louder than I intended to. Ashely noticed and turned away. "Well, try to relax."

"I heard you sigh."

I could only utter, "What?"

"I have to go, Larry."

I blew out a breath. "Get my pillow—"

Click.

Ashley whipped her head back to me and raised her perfectly plucked eyebrow. "Wow, that sucked."

I somehow managed to laugh. "Can this day be any more agonizing?"

She smiled eerily as her gaze shifted to a text. Ashley's expression changed. She looked anxious, scrutinizing it. Then she murmured, "My mom's having a meltdown, too." She took a slow breath, contemplating something. "I have to go." Her voice fell to a whisper. "One day, I'll tell you what it's like to grow up with a depressed mother who numbs her pain with alcohol."

Ashley fell silent as tears filled her eyes.

I took steps beside her, slipped an arm around her shoulder, and pulled her close. "Are you okay?"

She gave me a sad smile. "The possibility of a stay-at-home order has triggered her depression," she replied, wiping her eyes and walking away. "My mom and dad don't get along...."

My eyes dropped to the puddle of water on the floor as I fell into the office chair. I wanted to scream expletives, but what good would that have done? I felt a surge of disappointment, then anger. I snatched my phone off the desk when it pinged, assuming it was Allison, but of course, it had to be Tyler who suggested I sell The Gym again. I rubbed my face and checked on Ashley.

She texted back: I'm fucking fine. Worry about your own mess!

Alrighty then.

As I sat there, it dawned on me that I should remind my fiancée that I loved her. With a calming breath, I texted her my typical: I love you!

I expected to see her automatic, 'I love you more!'

But it never came.

CHAPTER ELEVEN

THE END OF AN ERA

FEBRUARY 26, 2020

THE GYM

Two days later, Aurora approached me with a concerned look.

"Boss, I'll teach a yoga class for anyone who wants to take it in March."

I sighed heavily. "That would most likely send our remaining members into a tizzy. I appreciate you, Aurora, but we better play along until we figure out this Health Emergency."

It was difficult to believe that all this bad stuff would eventually lead to something better. In forty-eight hours, my publisher postponed the release of my new novel to June. The CDC reported the first known case of the virus in California. Moreover, political polarization mounted as the media motivated the masses to call for the President to enforce a stay-at-home order.

Meanwhile, mayhem ensued at the fitness center when opposing political views caused a brawl between two oversensitive members.

After cleaning their blood off a spin bike, it appeared to be the dystopian nightmare that Carla wrote about in her book.

This wasn't George Orwell's *1984*. It was real-life's 2020.

A feeling of despair overwhelmed me. My heart was beating too fast as I staggered away from the TVs. I couldn't bear to watch The Monster sell America that regulations and corporate control would benefit the country. I tried to understand how *'We the People'* would buy this feeling of fear and hopelessness. The problem, it seemed, was that they believed the lies. I'd harbored so many emotions while pretending this couldn't happen; maybe I wasn't thinking straight.

How could anyone applaud this monster?

I walked into the office and wrote in my notepad:

Dystopia - feelings of fear - hopelessness - mandates - regulations - corporate control - bureaucratic control - an ideology enforced by the government.

Whenever I passed a TV with the incessant news, I thought about Carla. I would lie in bed, staring into the darkness, remembering her call. It haunted me. Aurora sensed my tension and entered the office to console me. I wanted to vent to her but couldn't utter a single word. As she tried to cheer me up, my smile flatlined when Allison texted me that she had taken the girls to her parents' house. After reading her text, my breaths were coming hard and fast.

I could tell she was still typing.

I waited.

I hate these dots!

Then came her follow-up: **Did you notice I cleaned the house?**

Appreciation and gratitude.

Before I could thank her, I was stunned by another text. It wasn't Allison; it was Ashley: **Carla's book will be out in two days!**

Where is she going to hide? I joked.

Ashley replied: **LOL!**

Immediately, I started typing a response to Allison but stopped when my eyes rolled at her follow-up: **You don't appreciate anything I do. I'm sick of doing EVERYTHING FOR EVERYONE!**

Call her. She's spiraling into a tizzy!

As it rang, I shook my head, trying to process everything. I made a mental list of her dusting, vacuuming, and organizing the kitchen pantry and was careful to include it all. But when she deliberately sent me to her voicemail, I hung up and cursed under my breath as Aurora quietly slipped out of the office.

My actions were as childish as Allison's.

I tossed my phone on the desk and contemplated dumping another water bottle on my head, but I took a calming breath instead. It was best to be practical, so I spent the next hour canceling new equipment orders.

A few hours later, at around 5:30, I received a call from Ashley. She had met a friend for happy hour at the Yacht Club and noticed Tyler hurrying down the dock. She stopped talking after she informed me that he had approached The Jolly Roger. All I heard was the wind off the river.

Finally, I said, "Ashley, what's happening?"

"Tyler boarded the boat and was greeted by Stuart."

"The Monster?"

"Yes."

"What are they doing?"

"Stuart's doing all the talking," she whispered. "Wait…he handed Tyler an envelope. I don't want them to see me here; I'll call you back—"

Click.

An hour later, Ashley informed me that she would feel Tyler out with a casual call about a mutual friend, but first, she sent me a string of texts. All the emotions she'd bottled up since reading Carla's manuscript came spilling out. There was no way to keep my distance from this.

At 7:00, Ashley texted me: **Are you still at The Gym?**

When I texted her that I was leaving, she responded that she was nervous because Carla wasn't answering her phone. Then Ashley almost hit me while pulling into The Gym's parking lot. Everything was moving fast now, including me. I rushed to her as she skidded to a stop in a parking space.

Ashley lowered her window. "Tyler didn't see me…he didn't," she said, convincing herself. "He rambled about his ruined career and Sharky's failing liver."

"Sharky wasn't well last month. Is he in the hospital?"

"I wanted to ask, but the call ended with a pounding on Tyler's door."

"What do you mean?"

Ashley glanced unevenly at me. "I mean, it wasn't a knock from a neighbor looking for butter." Her voice went to a whisper. "Larry, this is scary."

"Don't overreact."

My mind was racing with questions.

Why would Tyler, who loathed The Monster, want to meet him?

What was in the envelope?

Was Carla in grave danger?

God willing, she was still alive.

With everything on Ashley's mind, one thing kept rising to the surface; she should've called Carla from the Yacht Club to warn her that Tyler had met Stuart. I could tell Ashley assumed the worst. She hopped out of her jeep, not knowing whom to trust. Then she turned to me, and with a slight frown, she said, "Carla still hasn't answered. I called her four times."

I insisted that Tyler wouldn't harm Carla, but Ashley threw her hands up and swore that Tyler was desperate. She mentioned a scenario where he snapped because Carla decided to move on after their breakup. Ashley didn't believe that Tyler could live without Carla. She also knew that Stuart wanted Carla silenced and assumed that Tyler, who was desperate for money, had taken his cash to carry out the job of murdering her.

Ashley said, "Larry, I saw The Monster hand Tyler the envelope."

"You're jumping to a rather dramatic conclusion."

"You're refusing to see the reality of this."

"Carla's probably hiding because of her book."

Ashley looked up sharply, intensely eyeing me. "But did she get out before they got to her? I hate to ask, but do you know when Allison communicated last with Dr. Avery?"

I sighed, mindful that Dr. Strange had broken it off with Carla. "Allison told me that the doctor ended their relationship. I'm meeting her for dinner tomorrow." I forced a smile. "It's like we've been taking one step forward but two steps back lately."

She nodded, walking to her jeep. "So, date night's a big deal?"

"It shouldn't be, but it's been a strange couple of months."

Ashley opened her car door to leave but turned back to me and said, "I can't stop thinking about that psychic. I sent you Carla's manuscript. The next lockdown in her story would affect us." She paused, shaking her head. "Days from now, we'll know how right she is. Please start reading it when you get a free moment. You, too, will believe this is the end of an era."

I swallowed hard and walked back toward The Gym. My best move was to get as much done as I feasibly could in the meantime. Most importantly, this meant not letting myself get overwhelmed by the chaos swirling around me.

•   •   •

The following day, I was only focused on our much-needed date night. We decided to meet at The Fish House on Friday after work. Without discussing anything else, we gave each other a small, sad smile and went in different directions. She landed on the couch in the family room, turned on CNN, and tipped back a glass of wine as I sat at the kitchen table and opened my notepad. With a moan, I scribbled:

I am officially panicked, yet I must pretend I'm not. I won't survive a lockdown. The money I've spent on the fitness center upgrades will be due before....

I tossed my pen on the table when Allison raised the volume on Dr. Folie's Health Emergency update. I tried to steady my breathing.

Exhaling steadily, I sat in bewilderment, listening to every word that came out of the chief medical advisor's mouth.

Then, I shook my head, picked up the pen, and wrote:

Nothing about this feels right. Something deep inside me won't allow me to discredit my gut instinct. It's only fifty-seven days into the year, but it feels like six months. There is no way to embrace the uncertainty ahead.

For two months, I've taken notes as if I would write Carla's dark fairy tale as far-fetched fiction; however, with each passing day, it is becoming our reality.

Is the control we have over our lives an illusion?

There is nothing permanent except change.

Right now, my focus is on Allison, though. We need to reconnect. Tomorrow's date night is a big deal.

CHAPTER TWELVE

DATE NIGHT

FEBRUARY 28, 2020

THE FISH HOUSE

I met Allison at 6:00.

The server pointed to her at our favorite table overlooking the river. It was a beautiful evening, and as I walked over, she raised her eyes and looked up at me. I broke into a huge grin, dropped my forehead to the side of her head, and whispered in her ear. "You look stunning in the moonlight."

I kissed her.

My fiancée forced a smile, leaned back in her chair, and thought carefully about how to begin. I took a slow breath feeling anxious yet relieved we would finally be airing out our issues. But then, she said, "Everyone at school believes the country will lockdown." She paused and just stared at me. The feelings I saw in her eyes were more than what she could verbalize. I wanted to kiss her again: I should've kissed her, but I felt like I was on a slippery slope, sliding further away.

I hid my fear behind a quick, darting smile. "It's been difficult getting through each day. I want to talk about what we can control. Us."

"Larry, I'm talking about us. What are we going to do?"

I swallowed hard. "March will be tough."

A frown darted across her face. "March? Italy's locked down, and we're next."

"You don't know that."

Allison shook her head. "My depression has worsened," she said. "And a stay-at-home order will not help me. It won't help us—" she paused as Ashely's text pinged loudly.

I slid my phone off the table and read it: **You guys have a magical love! Enjoy date night.**

My heart ached. I shifted my gaze to Allison and asked, "Are you still talking to the doctor?"

Her mouth trembled. "Yes. Shawn reassures me that I'm not crazy."

I hesitated, not knowing if I would cry or curse her out but said, "And I don't?"

She shrugged. "Not lately."

"I wish you would put yourself in my shoes…." I stopped in mid-sentence as she turned toward the river.

She mumbled, "He understands my depression."

I didn't want to hear that, so I leaned forward, pretending I hadn't. "What?"

A few seconds later, Allison said, "It's not what you think."

"Can you explain it?"

She shook her head solemnly. "You wouldn't understand."

"Try me."

"Just know I was happy for a couple of years."

Her comment left me speechless. We had been inseparable since our first date. When we weren't together, we texted like teenagers, only interested in seeing each other again. Finally, I said, "Allison, we're an awesome couple. Members of The Gym believe that we have a magical love."

I figured she would take strength from that, but she said, "I'm not a romantic." I looked at my fiancée and saw that sad reflection in her eyes again. "For me, two years is a long time."

I smiled at the server who came over to fill our water glasses and whispered, "We're going to grow old together."

"I did think so," she replied contemplatively. "But since you finished your book, you've changed, and the uncertainty of this shitty year has me doubting everything."

I started to say something and realized I couldn't. I was avoiding the need to be introspective. When I opened my mouth to speak again, I only said, "I don't want to create any more barriers between us." Since I wasn't willing to delve into her depressed state or look into the mirror, I quickly added, "Your hands are shaking. Are you cold? Do you want to sit inside?"

Allison cupped her wine glass with both hands as if it were hot chocolate and took a sip. "My hands aren't shaking," she said defensively. She placed her glass back down and pulled her hands under the table. "You seek perfection—and I am far from being perfect."

The remark only further frustrated me because I couldn't deny that she had a valid point. I had been short with her during these moments of sadness when she was drinking. I couldn't recall feeling this way when she wasn't and shifted uncomfortably, trying to smile. "Honey, I am so grateful we met," I said quietly, reaching across the table, hoping she'd put her hand in mine. "I love you."

Her hands remained on her lap. "Real life is too ugly for you. And for your books."

"What does that mean?" I barked a bit too loudly. I took a breath. "What are you saying?"

"You love the fairy tale that you wrote."

"No, I love you."

"No, you're a hopeless romantic who was momentarily inspired."

"Inspired by our reality. Us, together." I grabbed my phone and scrolled through our pictures. "Look at all these amazing memories of us living, loving, and laughing, like very few people do...."

She steadied her hands and picked up her wine glass for another sip as if she didn't hear a word I said. "For a long time, you convinced me that we could work—I believed in your fairy tale."

Neither of us knew what to do next. We stared at each other for an awkward moment. For the first time, I questioned if our love could protect us from the ugliness of the world.

I swore it could.

But deep down, that wasn't the only problem.

And the ugliness had reared its hideous head.

After a longer sip of wine, she murmured, "You can't deal with my depression. It's not part of your happily ever after, Larry."

I couldn't take it anymore.

Allison began to sabotage our happiness after every third glass of wine. "It hasn't been your depression lately!" I exclaimed. "It's been the wine." I lowered my voice. "Your eyes are even bloodshot."

She shrugged. "My eyes are bloodshot because I've been crying."

I wanted to scream and jump into the river. Staying calm when she went dark was challenging, but I had to be empathetic. Curing her with a well-intentioned phrase wasn't the answer. When I apologized, her eyes closed tightly, and she went in a different direction when she opened them. "You don't get my profession. Every teacher drinks. We need some relief."

I released my breath with a heavy sigh. I didn't mean to; I couldn't help it. I felt like I would've exploded if I hadn't. "Allison, tell me what would help you."

"I just need a break from it all."

"So, let's go away next weekend."

"We can't spend frivolously right now."

We sounded like a broken record, repeating the same lines over and over. I felt there wasn't one moment that I could build on. Regardless, I continued, "If a weekend away allowed us to get back to the way things were, it would be well worth it."

"A weekend away won't help me. I'm not meant to be in a relationship. Not even with you. The love of my life...."

I stared at her; I was beyond exhausted.

The silence between us was broken by the rough river splashing against the rocks by the dock. I knew I should say something—the pain in her eyes was unmistakable. Her hands still shook when she reached for her glass as the server dropped off our fish tacos.

I tried to eat, but the silence tore at my nerves.

Then, Allison's gaze landed on Ashley's text as it came to my phone, ending our dinner.

Before tonight, it would have seemed impossible to think we would ever break up. But at that moment, life seemed different: As if anything were possible.

CHAPTER THIRTEEN

GONE GIRL!

MARCH 1, 2020

THE GYM

It was early afternoon.

The sea and sky were a solid sheet of sparkling blue. Sunlight glinted along the surface of the water. Today was no typical beach day, however. Aurora watched The Gym as I accompanied Ashley to the shoreline; that lazy Sunday was disrupted by the news that Carla was officially reported missing. More than once, Ashley said, "I should've called Carla when I saw Tyler with The Monster." Overwhelmed by guilt, she reached into her pocket, pulled out a joint, and lit up. She took a deep toke and held it behind her back. "Is that discreet enough?"

"Maybe to the two Canadians drowning in the cold surf," I smirked. "Not so much to the group behind us Snapchatting your drug habit from their beach chairs."

Ashley laughed. "Stop!"

I smiled, swaying with the sea breeze, but I was uneasy. Allison had served herself a glass of wine with every CNN Special Report. The news was a riptide of cold, dark water that repeatedly sucked her under. I rubbed my fingers across my brows, trying to make sense of her depression which was tied to Carla's dark fairy tale in too many ways.

With each passing day, it became apparent that there were too many political axes to grind. The Monster had been on every media outlet using technology as a fear-mongering tactic to force a stay-at-home order while ridiculing Trump's handling of the Health Emergency. The extent to which The Monster's hatred for Trump influenced the scientific discussion around the origins of this virus was now apparent. Scientists were lying. And the ones who told the truth were murdered or went missing.

In eight weeks, everything had changed. My bills were mounting as the fitness center's members were fleeing at an alarming rate. Meanwhile, my depressed fiancée kept her options open with a dispirited doctor who dated the missing woman who had me undeniably obsessed with an unbelievable storyline, rapidly playing out as the truth.

A dark fairy tale!

I was saying those words while visualizing a twisted book cover. My mind kept going back to this gain-of-function research. Given the astronomical risks, I wondered how it was even legal, so I presented the question to Tyler.

Ashley took another toke and nudged my arm.

"Someone texted you." I pulled my phone from my back pocket. Tyler felt that Carla was safe. Then I winced as his follow-up flashed with an answer. I read it while digging my bare feet in the sand: In 2017, the NIH Director, Dr. Frank Folie, argued that the benefits of gain-of-function research outweighed the pandemic risk. Carla found that to be a mind-boggling and incomprehensible position for an official charged with protecting the health of Americans. Since Folie's office declined to comment, Carla contacted one of her whistleblowers, who stated that Folie 'pushed' it through the White House without even the National Security Advisor knowing.

A moment later, a call jolted me.

I answered, "Hey, Aurora."

"Boss, the police have questions about Carla and Tyler's gym memberships."

My trembling hand pressed my phone against my ear. "We're heading back over the dune." I stepped into my flip-flops and glanced at Ashley as her beautiful face flushed. She put the joint out, popped a piece of gum in her mouth, and we crossed A1A in silence. We noticed police cars parked in front of The Gym.

Ashley tucked a stray lock of black hair around her ear and said, "Should I tell them about Tyler and Stuart on Hook's yacht?"

"Hold that thought," I said, eyeing two men in suits. "Something doesn't feel right."

Her dark eyes widened. "I've seen scenes like this on *Criminal Minds*. The FBI is taking over the investigation."

My eyebrow rose. "What?"

"The FBI took over because Tyler murdered Carla."

I shook my head. "He just texted me that he thought she was safe. I believe he knows she is."

Regardless of what I thought, Tyler had to be a person of interest. So, might Stuart, and Dr. Strange, for that matter. I thought about Allison. I wanted to call her, but the detectives were waiting to question me. As we walked into The Gym, one stuck out his hand. I shook his hand and assessed him. He was a tall man with a paunch, probably from too many days behind a desk. His head was slightly thrust forward as his dark brown eyes took in Ashley.

"I'm Detective John Franks." He smiled at her. "Your daughter's beautiful."

At that moment, Ashley took a few steps forward, amused. "I'm not his daughter."

"No, that's Ashley…an acquaintance…a gym member. I'm Larry. I own the fitness center—"

Ashley interjected, "Larry's also a writer. I read his books."

The detective's eyes narrowed to tiny slits as his gaze shifted from me to her and back to me. Finally, he said, "I'm with the Melbourne Beach police department. Do you know Carla Kimbrel and Tyler Harrison?"

"Yes."

"Are they members?"

"No."

"They were seen leaving The Gym together the night she disappeared."

"By whom?"

The detective pointed into the parking lot and asked, "Do you know the man talking to the agents?" I turned and winced. It was Whibbles, a long-time member who calls The Gym every morning asking for me, the leader. Whibbles was one of those who was hard to discern if he was screwing with you when he blurted out obscene remarks or sounds, always randomly in the oddest places. No one quite knew his true identity.

"Yes…why?"

"He called the missing person hotline with information that led us here."

I gave the detective a smile that said he knew better, and I calmly replied, "His name is Whibbles. He isn't playing with a full deck."

"He also told us he's a member."

"A member who walks backward on the treadmills making bird calls."

The detective looked startled, even alarmed, as he walked outside. After a brief sidebar with the agents, I informed him of my conversation with Tyler at Charlie & Jakes. He wasn't moved. The veteran detective glared at me and said, "Love makes people do crazy things."

Startled, I glanced at Ashley, who nodded in agreement.

•   •   •

The following day, Monday, FBI agents returned to The Gym. Their abrupt exit after the Whibbles incident made no sense to me, but I became suspicious when they returned before my scheduled shift. I might not have second-guessed that part if they hadn't found Carla's knapsack on the locker room bench. But they had.

I took a quick shower and headed over.

When I arrived, the agents were gone. Aurora informed me they were looking for witnesses. There were none. Nor was there any chance that Carla's knapsack was in The Gym on Sunday. I had repositioned the women's locker room bench when I vacuumed. There was nothing on it.

At 10:00 a.m., a fit FBI agent with gray slicked-back hair handed me his card. He introduced himself as Agent Adam Harper. He knew my name and asked me when Carla had interviewed me for my upcoming book release. He seemed startled when I told him the exact date considering it was two months ago. He assumed we frequently spoke when I admitted it was a date etched in my mind.

Agent Harper shot me a cold smile. "What was your last conversation about?"

I certainly couldn't go there, so I cleared my throat. "Well, it's been a while," I confessed. "Carla dated a doctor who talks to my fiancée." I paused, thinking about how to word the rest. "Carla stopped communicating with me because she believed that the love story part of my book was overstated."

He had a scowl in his eyes. "So…Carla's jealous of your fiancée—"

"She was upset that her boyfriend still talks to my fiancée."

"What's her name?"

"Allison Tinke."

He blinked. "Why would Carla interview you for a book she didn't get?"

"She did get it. Carla found out afterward that her boyfriend talks to Allison."

Agent Harper asked, "When you met with Carla's boyfriend, did you know he was talking to Allison?"

"I met with Carla's ex, Tyler Harrison," I replied. "I've never met the doctor."

"Tyler's not the doctor?"

"No," I said.

"What is the doctor's name?"

"Shawn Avery."

Agent Harper seemed confused. After a lengthy conversation with the agents who examined the contents of Carla's knapsack, he came back with proof that Carla was dating Tyler. I wiped my forehead, quickly realizing that I sounded like I was deliberately misleading them. Then I immediately told Harper that the doctor had broken things off with Carla, but it was too late.

Agent Harper said, "We found a red knapsack in the locker room. It has pages of Carla's diary."

This woman is something else!

I cleared my throat. "Well, that must've been entertaining."

"Are you being sarcastic?" he asked impatiently.

I sighed. "I'm frustrated."

He continued, "Carla wrote that she dated a volatile man named Tyler Harrison. The email associated with her phone turned up active accounts on TikTok, Snapchat, Instagram, and Facebook, proving that they were a couple."

A feeling of lightheadedness came over me. "You found Carla's phone?"

"Yes."

I blinked suspiciously. When I googled Dr. Avery, I recalled that Carla had no Facebook account. My mind raced back to Caroline's associates stating that Carla was on Facebook with him. Maybe Caroline was setting me up. Although I couldn't confirm anything, I swallowed hard, concerned that this nightmare liaison with a twist of abduction would lead to Allison.

Why would it matter?

My thoughts were frantic. Agent Harper waited for me to enlighten him, so I said, "Carla hasn't returned to The Gym since the interview. Someone placed that knapsack here." I sat at the security monitor but couldn't view the footage that would've proved it. "Give me a second, please. It's an old system—"

"Larry," he interrupted. "It's Carla's diary. We've verified she dated Tyler Harrison—"

"With all due respect, you also took Whibbles seriously." I was jumpy and rechecked Carla's Facebook page. To my surprise, I found it—with no privacy settings. Carla had current pictures with Tyler for the world to see. But not one of Dr. Strange.

Agent Harper continued, "Larry, have you and Carla had romantic relations?"

"No, I know how this appears. But we haven't communicated since a few days after her interview." My voice rose. "What did Tyler tell you?"

"He confirmed they dated—"

"Yes, but when?" I asked, contemplating pulling up Carla's manuscript.

Thankfully, Agent Harper took a call, and I took a much-needed breath. Three long minutes later, he came back. Tyler denied that Carla ever dated Dr. Strange. He claimed he only knew his name from Carla's research for her book. I shook my head, wishing I hadn't deleted the screenshots Caroline texted me.

I had nothing. I sank into the office chair spinning as Agent Harper left a voicemail for my fiancée. Shortly after that, the agents left. Gripping my phone, I called Allison, but that call went to voicemail too. I could barely set my phone down when Ashley hurried into the office. I asked her if she was on social media with Carla or Tyler. She confirmed she'd been on Snapchat and Instagram with Tyler. I deliberated for a moment and turned to the security footage again, trying to understand what had happened.

"I'm going to find out who dropped that knapsack in the locker room," I said. "It makes no sense that it would be left here."

"Not unless someone wants you to be involved," Ashley chirped, "I'll get the wine."

"We might need some popcorn."

Ten minutes later, she returned with both. "Any clues?"

"It rebooted to last week."

An hour after that, I realized this would be a tedious task. I fast-forwarded days of periodic check-ins due to the Health Emergency but found nothing. Then, just after we opened, I noticed a lady wearing a baseball hat and sunglasses with a knapsack. She hurried by the check-in counter and slowed down, walking by the last camera. I confirmed the date: Monday, March 2, 2020. It was this morning at 6:04.

Finally!

A chill went up my spine. The lady entered The Gym, dropped the knapsack in the locker room, and disappeared. She must've exited through the back door as the morning shift retrieved our mail. When I rewound the footage, Ashley pointed out that the lady was wearing a wig.

My mind raced back to the interview. Carla was roughly the same height and build. I turned to Ashley. "I know it's blurry, but that looks like Carla."

She stared at the monitor. "It also looks like Lauren Bacall."

I looked at Ashley. "Who?"

"Wait, no. Maybe. I have a bunch of friends about that size."

I sighed heavily, "Right."

"What are you thinking?"

I made a gesture of dismissal and noted, "That's a blue knapsack. The one the FBI found was red."

Her brow arched suspiciously. "But isn't that the end?"

I nodded. "Yes, I'm going home. I desperately need to sleep."

"I'll see you tomorrow."

I nodded again and shifted my gaze back to the monitor.

As Ashley walked out, I realized the red knapsack must've been inside the blue one. There are no cameras in the back hallway; Carla could've easily pulled the red one out and taken the blue one with her. I thought about it for a moment. Why didn't she come in the back door completely undetected?

This person wanted to be seen. I advanced the footage frame by frame, searching for a clue. She slowed down and unzipped her sweatshirt, steps from disappearing off camera. I paused the footage and zoomed in on her. She was deliberately revealing a Florida Gator T-shirt. It was the same one Carla wore when she interviewed me. "That's Carla," I whispered to myself. "She wanted me to see her because she still wants me to write this story. Something changed her mind."

Carla was embarrassed that she had overreacted.

Instead of apologizing, she decided to play games.

Why else would she have had Ashley read her manuscript?

I rubbed my face and texted Ashely: **How did Carla know you were my Beta-reader?** I leaned back in the chair, impatiently waiting for her response.

A minute later, it flashed up: **Tyler knows the server, which I let read The Gym. Remember Hannah? You met her at Charlie & Jakes.**

One thing was sure—Carla had my attention.

I placed my phone back on the desk as my eyes narrowed at a red envelope in the mail. I leaned forward and snatched it out of the stack. The envelope was mailed at the end of January and addressed to Peter Pan Man, not The Gym.

I cursed out loud. "Fucking unreal!" I could still hear Carla's voice the day she interviewed me: *Peter Pan Man needs to be added to the titles of your books.*

Breathe.

With a couple of deep breaths, I placed two photocopied pages on the desk and smoothed them with my hands. I felt a weird sense of déjà vu, as if I'd been thrown back in time to look at the days following Carla's call through her diary. And so, I read:

Thursday – January 16, 2020

Dear Diary,

Peter Pan Man is more of a salesman than a romantic. His fiancée, Allison Tinke, has been texting my boyfriend. Shawn and Allison dated the same summer I met Tyler. Ironically, it was when this dark fairy tale began. I can't deal with any more lies. When I asked to see Shawn's texts to Allison, he told me he deleted them because he had warned her about the lab leak.

Confidential information, I had thought he only shared with me. He confessed he was drunk and upset. Now I'm drunk and upset.

Friday – January 17, 2020

Whistleblower #4 sends emails proving that the EH Alliance received millions of dollars from The Monster to study bat coronaviruses in the Wuhan, China, lab accused of either accidentally or intentionally leaking this virus.

My thoughts shifted back to a conversation with Allison when she mentioned the EH Alliance. It was right after Dr. Strange texted her. Then I checked my notes and found an article that tied The Monster to this organization.

The EH Alliance is a U.S.–based non-government organization that aims to protect people, animals, and the environment from emerging infectious diseases. The nonprofit is focused on research that seeks to prevent pandemics. The organization's ties with the Wuhan Institute of Virology were questioned following the outbreak.

And I jumped back into Carla's diary.

Saturday – January 18, 2020

Whistleblower #5 stated that The Monster had a biologist ally threaten to squash a paper on this lab-leak theory from a public preprint server.

Dinner with Shawn at Ember and Oak was nice. He apologized for his communication with Allison. He admitted he was struggling with his depression and insisted she had been as well. I understood it as what they had in common. Shawn claimed it was the reason he didn't want to end their friendship. He also believed in whistleblower #5! Five former EHA staff members know of an orchestrated effort to kill the lab-leak theory because of The Monster.

Monday – January 20, 2020

In one State Department meeting, officials seeking to demand transparency from the Chinese government said colleagues explicitly told them not to explore the Wuhan Institute of Virology's gain-of-function research because it would bring unwelcome attention to the U.S. government who funded it.

Wine time with Michelle was irritating. She swore Shawn initiated contact with Allison. Sorry…not buying it, Cruella! You showed your true colors today, and I don't do green with envy.

Tuesday – January 21, 2020

My book is almost complete! I might be disappearing in the not-so-distant future.

And the plot thickens.

When I cleared my head and calmed my anger, I wrote:

Gone Girl!

CHAPTER FOURTEEN

DOWN THE RABBIT HOLE

MARCH 5, 2020

THE HOUSE

The doorbell rang. Then came three hard knocks.

I hurried to the door. "Who is it?" I asked.

"It's Carla." I was too surprised to answer. "Larry," she continued. "This is no time to be upset."

"How did you find me?"

"I followed your second star to the right, ya silly goose!" I thrust open the door. Carla shrugged, wearing a white T-shirt and blue jeans with designer holes.

"Why are you haunting me?" I asked.

She smiled eerily. My gaze shifted to some distorted trees and children laughing. And a rabbit. I took a step outside and watched the rabbit hop into a hole. I rubbed my eyes. The children were all boys.

Lost Boys.

Then the faint scent of cigarette smoke wafted over me with the morning breeze. I turned back to Carla. "Did the Lost Boys come with you?"

"No, they came with your imagination, Peter." She smirked. "Stay focused. You must take me to the firm."

My heart thumped, out of beat. "No! Your interview was a farce. You disappear and reappear. You dropped a knapsack off in The Gym, knowing I would see you. You send me pages of your diary. Now you want me to take you to Hook's firm?"

Her eyes pinned me. "I need your help, but you need mine, too. So, please hurry."

At that point, I couldn't answer. I just went to grab my keys. She was in the passenger seat when I got to my car. Carla questioned if the American public would ever find out about The Monster's ties to the research done at the Wuhan laboratories. She lit another cigarette, took a long drag, and said, "The President treasured January's trade deal with China. He refused to see that they were using this virus to their strategic advantage. He has no idea how many D.C. bureaucrats are involved in this cover-up." She paused as ash blew on the dashboard and explained. "China is obsessed with dangerous viruses. In twelve years, China's virologists have discovered two thousand new viruses, while over the past two hundred years, the rest of the world has only discovered two-thousand-two hundred and eighty-four."

"I know. I'm reading your book," I said, staring into my rearview mirror. My vision was going a little hazy from the adrenaline or maybe from the panic I felt. "Are we being followed?"

Carla flicked her cigarette out the window and turned around.

"No. I don't know. Maybe," she said. Her voice was meek and confused. "Can you drive faster?"

I sensed her distress. "No, I can't. I don't understand why this is happening."

"Sometimes terrible things happen to change our lives for the better."

I sighed heavily. "My life was moving along swimmingly until I met you."

"Not true." Her eyes were as firm as her voice. "You were drifting away from Allison."

I was surprised by her statement. "What?"

"All the best love stories have one thing in common, Larry."

"What's that?"

"You must go against the odds to get to the happily ever after."

I glanced at her sideways. "What are you saying?"

"I made a mistake. When Shawn left my life, I found out that you and Allison have something quite rare—an extraordinary love. A magical love."

"You're confusing me even more."

She grinned. "I'm talking about your next book," she said. "I see a dark fairy tale with a monster, mayhem, and a true…magical love which is tested in ways that are difficult to imagine."

I blinked, thinking. "You told Tyler that."

She nodded. "I also reminded Tyler that gratitude unlocks the fullness of life. Is it possible you've taken Allison for granted lately?"

I opened my mouth, but no words came out. My mind raced back to our date night at The Fish House.

Then a text pinged Carla's phone. After muttering a litany of obscenities, she looked up. "Larry, pull into the backlot." I took a hard right. The security guard wasn't at the gate, and it was up. She smiled. "Tyler did it."

I gasped, "Tyler?"

She pointed to a parking spot. "Park there."

"I'm not parking!"

"Please!" I swung into the spot and turned to face her. "You must go with me."

Don't go.

DON'T GO!

DON'T YOU DARE GO!

Carla beckoned me with her eyes.

"Fuck it," I muttered. "Let's go."

I followed her into the firm. My whole body tingled, but I was meant to be there. Carla hurried ahead of me, grabbed the door, opened it, and I ran inside. The hallway was dark and cooler than it should've been. We walked down the hallway and stopped at The Monster's office. Carla opened the door and pulled me in as she made a call. "I'm in."

A man's voice replied, "He knows. You have thirty seconds."

She put the call on speaker, placed her phone down, and rummaged through The Monster's desk drawer. I could hear the panic in her breathing. "Tyler…it's gone."

Silence.

Her voice was frantic. "Answer me—"

A chill moved up my spine. Carla murmured something very softly. It might have been *Christ.*

Then everything happened in slow motion. Her body quivered as she slumped over and fell to the floor. The gunshot came from the hallway and was silenced. I saw nothing. I stared in horror. Carla's face was all shadows, but her blood had pooled into a puddle. "Larry…."

I knelt beside her. "Carla, stay with me!"

She grabbed my arm. "The couples that are meant to be are the ones who go through everything designed to tear them apart and come out stronger." Carla shook my arm.

Then my eyes flickered open to Allison. "You were dreaming," she said.

I hesitated. "I believe I fell down the rabbit hole."

"With Carla?"

"No, my dream was about us…."

"My name isn't Carla," Allison snapped, marching away. "Try again."

I rubbed my face and followed her. "Allison, you're the one texting men late at night."

"Don't spin this on me. Besides, Ashley's constantly texting you."

"She's my beta reader." I sighed: I shook my head and tried again. "Listen, the dream came with a meaningful message—"

"I don't care," she said. "We're good in bed…but honestly, that's all this has been for too long."

Anger crept into my voice. "How can you say that?"

"What's my favorite sex position?"

I stared at her. She could see my frustration, but she didn't care. "You're seriously doing this?"

"My favorite sex position is being loved and treated like a priority. How's that for a meaningful message?" Allison slammed the bathroom door and turned on the shower.

Twenty minutes later, she left for school without saying goodbye.

I scribbled on my notepad:

All the best love stories have one thing in common. You must go against the odds to get there.

I shook my head; I couldn't deny that Carla had been right about too much of this. And now, like the whistleblowers, she was gone. There was no way to confirm anything. And that seemed to be the plan.

Hours later, I called Agent Harper to inform him about Tyler's meeting with Stuart.

By 6:00 that evening, it checked out to be a legitimate sports memorabilia transaction with an invoice and pictures of Tyler's autographed baseballs in Stuart's sports bar to prove it.

I recalled Tyler's text, desperate to sell me his memorabilia. Then I sighed, seized by doubt.

CHAPTER FIFTEEN

THIS WORLD HAS GONE CRAZY

MARCH 10, 2020

THE GYM

It was five days later.

As the virus heated up, the FBI's investigation went cold. You would think a missing person case involving an attractive blonde in her thirties would have had Carla Kimbrel gaining national notoriety. But at this moment in time, the media was focused on an even bigger story: A GLOBAL PANDEMIC!

For a murder case, this was a worst-case scenario. But this couldn't have been better scripted for a writer exposing a GLOBAL CONSPIRACY. There were no new leads, tips, background information, or any reported sightings of Carla.

Agent Harper walked into The Gym on a call at 9:00 that Monday morning. Immediately, I discerned two things about this visit: One, there wouldn't be any more questions about Carla, and two, he knew the country would be on lockdown. He paced while on the call, gnawing on his fingernails. When it ended, he cast his eyes downward. In a hushed tone, he said, "We're done here. Thanks for your time." He bobbed his square chin. "Good luck with your business."

A gust of breath escaped me, but I didn't speak.

After he left, I went to call Allison but cradled my phone against my chest. I realized that mentioning Carla would not have been a wise move. Aurora swore our arguing meant we still cared enough to fix what was broken. Regardless, I felt ungrounded and walked into the office, slightly dazed.

Ten minutes later, Ashley dropped her elbows on The Gym's check-in counter. "I just got a server job, and the restaurant cut my hours," she said, exasperated. "Can you believe this?"

I spun my chair with the office landline pressed to my ear. "Yes, please cancel the T-shirt order."

Ashley made her way into the office. "The country is shutting down."

"No," I said into the phone. "I don't have the confirmation number." She fell into the chair across from me. I raised a hand, still on the call. "No. Right now, things are too uncertain." I shook my head at Ashley checking her teeth in the reflection of her phone screen. "Thank you, goodbye." I set the phone back on the desk charger, and it rang. I picked it back up, glanced at the caller ID, and tossed it on the desk.

"Whibbles?" Ashley said. I nodded. She looked at me. "Any Carla updates?"

I wanted to scream out that Carla wasn't murdered, but I only drew a calming breath as she rambled about a rumor that they found her phone without a body. When I informed Ashley that the FBI was not buying that this was a murder case, she brought up a *Criminal Minds* episode where the body was chopped up and taken out in pieces. I looked at her as if she was speaking Martian. I wanted to believe I hadn't heard her right and looked to end the conversation.

"Ashley, stop!" I pleaded. "Tyler sold his sports memorabilia to Stuart. That's why The Monster handed him an envelope of money. Okay?"

"And you believe that?"

"Tyler asked me if I wanted to buy the jerseys weeks before. I still have the text."

Ashley frowned at me. "Jeez, I don't think we'll ever find out what happened." She grabbed a TV remote and jumped up. "Everyone is acting crazy."

I slumped in the office chair, unmotivated to do anything.

A moment later, a grouchy voice startled us.

"You're the owner."

Now what?

I stood up and faced the older gentleman. "How can I help you?"

"You can stop spreading a deadly disease!" he barked. "You damn fool."

With a quiet sigh, I reminded the man that there were no reported cases in the county while explaining that we were following the government guidelines. He refused to hear anything and insisted I cancel his wife's membership.

I took a slow breath and asked, "What's her name?"

"Nancy Neiman." My stomach knotted. The man continued, "You owe her money."

I walked over to him. As calmly as possible, I informed him I did not owe his wife anything. He waved his index finger at me, swearing she had already paid for March. When I showed him that she sold her friends the fifteen day-passes I gave her, he backed against the door, speechless.

"I have tried my best to appease Nancy," I stated, "I'm done. Anything else?"

The man looked astonished. His hand shook as he pulled the door open. "No. But I will sue you." He pushed a shopping cart full of toilet paper that he'd left outside across the parking lot, stuffed it into a brand-new BMW, and drove off.

Ashley hurried over. "What has gotten into everyone these days?" Her brown eyes widened with a look of confusion. "And what's with the rush on toilet paper?"

I shrugged. "The media must be reporting that this virus gives you diarrhea."

Ashley giggled momentarily and hit my arm. "Here comes another one."

Our heads tilted in disbelief at an older lady passing the fitness center with her shopping cart full of toilet paper. She glared at us and headed toward the parking lot. Soon after, there were a few more. I shook my head and called the grocery store. The manager, Mike, answered with commotion in the background. "Larry, I'm going to have to call you back. I have mayhem on the toilet paper aisle."

"Mike, do you know why?" I put the call on speaker.

"I don't know anything anymore—"

Click.

I leaned into Ashely and whispered, "Every day is a new level of crazy."

"Yup," she confirmed. "It certainly is."

We collapsed in the office chairs. I snatched up my notepad and flipped through the pages. "Why am I having dreams about everything in the world failing and love prevailing?"

"Perhaps it has something to do with what you're trying to write."

I sighed. "What?"

She grabbed my notepad out of my hands and began reading. "Dystopia. Corruption. Monsters. Mayhem. But not enough love." She tossed it on my lap. "Maybe it came too easy." She shrugged. "You're welcome."

"Defeating the monsters amidst all this mayhem is the story."

"Nope," she said. "You have more in common with Carla than you want to admit."

I slid down in the chair, crossed my arms, and shook my head. "Please don't say that."

The avid reader stood up to drive her point home. "Carla's life hasn't gone as she hoped, but deep down, she knows the world needs more fairy tales. Stories that remind us that good can prevail over evil." She paused and smiled at me. "And that love will conquer all, always. It would help if you cleared your head. Because to get this, you must love your Tink exactly as she is. When women feel appreciated in their own essence, they are empowered…."

I frowned. "I love Allison as she is."

"Lately, you haven't shown it. I eavesdropped on you, upset she left the oven on after cooking dinner. And when you were angry, she lost her debit card. And when she hit your car backing out of the driveway."

A wave of dizziness swept over me. I felt the blood draining from my head. I could see Ashley's mouth moving, but she was no longer talking to me. A middle-aged man who recently joined The Gym was at the check-in counter. He was a paramedic named Jeff. I took a sip of water and slowly pushed myself out of the chair as Ashley questioned him.

"Why don't you watch the news?"

Jeff gave a stern shake of his head. "Stuart Grossman and the media are scaring everyone stupid. It's the reason this fitness center's empty, with no reported cases in this county."

Ashley continued, "What about all the science talk?"

"I believe in science," Jeff said. "But fear-mongering and manipulating data are not, in any way, related to science. More virus deaths will occur when hospitals and medical professionals receive money for deaths related to this virus. There will certainly be a lack of transparency in the coming months—"

Ashley interrupted him, "Carla wrote about that."

"Who is Carla?"

"A writer who wrote a book on this."

Jeff nodded. "I have friends in Italy who have never seen bodies stacked in container trucks. The media is spinning a narrative to lock this country down and slow the economy."

"How can this happen?"

"The problem stems from a U.S. establishment that vacillates between apathy and alarmists," Jeff replied. "In an election year, that's dangerous. Fake news gets better ratings than real news." He paused and took a breath. "Sorry, I should keep my political views to myself."

Ashley's lips parted in shock. "What have you heard about the lockdown?"

Jeff's eyes widened as he looked at me. "I heard schools and fitness centers would close," he said. "But liquor stores and the big retail chains would remain open." He paused, drew his eyebrows apart in regret, and added. "Larry, I didn't mean to upset you. No one knows for sure. Please understand that."

I tried to ignore my aching head and think logically. I disregarded Tyler's texts and shunned Allison's concerns about The Gym closing. I felt groggy, like I woke up from a nightmare, hungover, and realized it was real.

Finally, I uttered, "Do you believe this will turn into a global pandemic?"

"Yes. People will be isolated, drinking more, exercising less, and living in fear. Mental illness and addiction will be a serious topic of conversation moving forward."

In an eerie silence, I swallowed hard, worried about Allison.

Then Ashley exclaimed, "This is crazy!"

Jeff nodded. "It is." He sighed. "This world has gone crazy."

CHAPTER SIXTEEN

THE DAY THAT CHANGED EVERYTHING

MARCH 11, 2020

THE GYM

On Wednesday afternoon, the WHO declared this mysterious virus outbreak a pandemic.

I sat in the office, planted my elbows on my wide-spread knees, and listened to the news; I was beyond distraught. There was plenty of sorrow to go around The Gym on this day as Aurora answered calls, scribbling down more member cancellations.

About twenty minutes later, I pushed myself up and paced the yoga studio. I learned that the WHO defined a pandemic as the 'worldwide spread' of a new disease. An outbreak is the occurrence of disease cases above what's typically expected, whereas an epidemic is more than an average number of cases of an illness in a region. This virus had found a foothold on every continent except for Antarctica.

In an Oval Office address, the President announced that he was restricting travel from Europe to the U.S. to slow the spread of the disease. Questions about how long The Gym could remain open were debated by the few members still lifting weights. It was a conversation Aurora saved me from when she yelled, "Ashley called you!"

I hurried away, grabbed my phone off the desk, and headed to my bench to call her back. Ashley answered on the second ring. "You know the librarian interview I was so excited about?"

I took a breath and exhaled. "Yes."

"It's been canceled. The library has removed the position because of the pandemic."

I straightened up, arching my back full of stress. "I feel your pain."

"I'm sorry. I know you have much more to lose. Is anyone at The Gym?"

"A few guys are lifting weights, wondering when we're closing. We're only averaging twenty check-ins a day. I had to take my employees' shifts."

The conversation ended when Allison called me. "Hey," I answered.

"Hey, Stuart Grossman is donating laptops to the children who can't afford one."

I blinked, stunned. "Excuse me?"

"His donations will allow all our kids to attend Zoom classes and learn from home."

I hesitated. "Whom is he trying to bribe now?"

Allison ignored my sarcastic reply and continued, "My principal speaks highly of him."

"Allison, Stuart's ex, refers to him as a monster."

She sighed. "Carla? Please don't go there. Besides, you should know that the media is mocking scientists who've suggested a lab leak." She lowered her voice. "Regardless of the truth, don't bring up any conspiracy theories. You could lose the few members you have left."

"Aren't you a little curious as to why these supposedly objective journalists are so quick to attack anyone who speaks about a lab leak?"

"No, I view it that they all agree the virus came from a wet market."

I sighed. "Well, I can't keep insisting that Carla's book is fiction while it plays out in real life."

"So, now you believe this was the day when fact became stranger than fiction?"

I stared at the date on my phone: Wednesday, March 11, and said, "Yes, I do."

"My principal's calling me. I have to go—"

Click.

•   •   •

As schools shifted to online learning, there was little doubt that Americans were becoming increasingly divided about the best way to proceed. Many Americans thought that strong lockdowns were the best idea moving forward. Although vaccines were many months away, the mainstream media preached that the economy should stay shut down by law until plans were further developed.

On the other hand, conservatives thought that the country's overall quality of life demanded that people make their own decisions about whether it's safe to go out in public and conduct business openly. Certain members of The Gym, like Aurora, insisted they would be worse off if they weren't fulfilling their exercise routines while maintaining a safe distance from others and frequently washing their hands. It seemed to be common sense in a world shaken to its core.

The following Saturday, Allison entered The Gym. When her eyes made it to mine, my anxiety seeped from me. She looked like she felt sad for me. I dropped my forehead to hers.

"Thanks for coming," I said quietly.

We took a step back and stared at each other with watery eyes.

A moment later, Aurora chirped, "I had a dream we stayed open. So, stop crying!"

Perhaps, that was an unrealistic dream, although I held on tight to it all weekend.

On Monday, the Governor ordered bars and nightclubs to close immediately, with fitness centers to follow by mid-week.

CHAPTER SEVENTEEN

THE YACHT CLUB CELEBRATION

MARCH 25, 2020

THE GYM

My business closed that Wednesday afternoon.

I locked the doors, turned from my dark fitness center, and squinted into the bright sunlight. For a moment, I couldn't breathe evenly. I collapsed on my bench and read a text from Allison. Her family had concerns about the future of The Gym amidst a global pandemic. I wasn't prepared to talk about it, but I dialed her anyway. My jaw tensed until the call rang to voicemail.

Slowly I leaned back on my bench. The humming waves momentarily consoled me. I breathed in the warm air as my gaze shifted beyond the dunes. I struggled to keep my eyes open, watching fluffy white clouds drift lazily across the blue sky in a gentle sea breeze.

I dozed off and heard a car horn.

Straightening awkwardly, I eyed a Jetta pulling up to The Gym. I pressed my hand against my forehead, hoping the person would feel sorry for me and keep going, but the car stopped.

I know this kid.

Paul Maxwell, an old employee, hopped out. "Hey, Larry, how are ya?"

"Oh, I'm just faking that everything will be okay to get through the day. How are you, Paul?"

The lanky young man smiled. "I'm good. I'd shake your hand, but I hear we're not supposed to do that anymore."

I paused, unsure if I should nod or laugh, and stood up instead. "What brings you out in a pandemic?"

He explained that Ashley came by his house when he returned from FSU and told him I was writing again. Glancing around the empty parking lot, he confessed that his brother had information to re-energize my storyline.

I drew in a breath and unlocked The Gym. As we entered, I asked. "Is your brother still Hook's accountant?"

"No, he left the firm because of Hook's business partner."

My breath caught in my throat. "Stuart Grossman...."

Paul peered outside. He appeared to be increasingly anxious. "Yes, Carla Kimbrel's ex—The Monster." As it turned out, Paul's brother resigned after Stuart replaced three long-time employees with the children of Beijing's party bosses. When the FBI questioned his brother, he knew the tech titan was guilty of more than he cared to know. Because of Ashley, Paul knew that Carla had interviewed me. He took a few steps along the wall, taking in member photos. "Man, I hope Carla's okay," he said. "When was the last time you spoke to her?"

My heart thumped in my chest. "Days after the interview. Before Carla found out that my fiancée was close to a doctor she dated."

He nodded as if he knew that Carla dated Dr. Strange but said, "Tyler Harrison."

"No. A doctor named Shawn Avery."

Paul stared oddly at me with his mouth ajar before claiming he had no idea. As he averted my glare, I could tell he was lying. "Anyway," he continued. "My brother has a friend working on a vaccine." I could tell from the raw edge of his voice he was serious. "First, they must determine which species of lock the virus key was best designed to unlock."

I rubbed the back of my neck. "You lost me."

"I'll put it this way; it wasn't any animal. Strangely, humans came out at the very top of the list."

"What does that mean?"

"The animal host from which the virus had been transmitted should have been at the top of the list. But it was humans."

A rush of adrenaline surged through my body. "Hold on a second," I breathed out. I opened my notepad and scribbled some notes. "Does your brother know Carla?"

Paul's face registered shock. "Yes, um…sure," he babbled nervously. "My brother heard disturbing things at the firm, confirming much of what Carla wrote. He wants to help her—"

"He knew about her research?"

"Yes. He's heard conference calls that linked Stuart to Dr. Frank Folie, Big Pharma, and Caroline Haines' contacts. Ashley told me Caroline made it into your book."

I nodded. "Yes. But having nothing to do with this. What did your brother hear?"

"He heard that the vaccines play a huge part in this pandemic—to the tune of one hundred billion dollars. Stuart's brother had worked at the lab in question. Certain individuals at the firm believe The Monster first came to Florida because his brother had threatened to expose their despicable plan. Now his brother is dead."

"A boating accident…right?"

"It was back in the summer of 2017," he said quietly. "Rumors spread that Stuart used Hook to get rid of his brother. The Monster wanted it to look like a love triangle that turned deadly."

"But they never found his body."

Paul nodded.

I continued, "What are your brother's thoughts about Caroline?"

"He believes she'll eventually be devastated."

"How so?"

He pulled a folded piece of paper from his back pocket. "Caroline received a page from Carla's diary. My brother got this from the snitch at the firm. Read it for yourself."

Sunday - October 13, 2019

Dear Diary, I've missed you!

So many emotions flooded me as my panties hit the floor: excitement, anger, irritation, desire, and fear. With Stuart, there was always fear. I accepted his invitation to dinner, knowing he'd planned on charming me out of writing the story he refused to have told. But let me back up. I haven't been updating you with all the details of my life lately because I've been busy.

The truth is that I've also been writing about Tyler. I created a fictional Tyler and called him Josh. I was afraid I wouldn't be able to hide how much I missed him. I needed a distraction—and sex. Then Stuart came knocking. Only this time, I used him. I fucked him. Blew him. And convinced him that I would stop writing this story. And it has haunted me more and more with each passing day. Oh, yeah, and then, when the time is right, this diary entry will end up in Caroline's inbox. It took me longer than I planned, but I'll get even with her too.

After dinner, we went back to Stuart's condo in Vero. He spilled some vintage Veuve on the floor while taking off his pants. If I weren't so horny, I would've gone for a shower at this point because touching him was unforgivable. Standing naked beside my bra and panties, I took a deep breath for courage. And that was that. He kissed my breast. I grabbed his tiny dick, and suddenly, I was straddling him on the bed. He moaned like he hadn't been fucked since I left him. I closed my eyes, envisioning Tyler, and a couple of minutes later, a whimper escaped my lips. I slowed the pace and carefully slid off him. The monster moaned louder—an angry moan. I crawled down on him and swallowed him whole. I could feel him ready to come, so I gently took his balls in my free hand and choked on his semen. I wiped my mouth, and he smiled his sinister smile as I walked out with an uncomfortable distaste for my life.

I stared at her words, craving a shower. Then I handed the page back to Paul and rubbed my face. "I'm not sure what Stuart will think is worse, her research or diary entries."

His eyes fell on her words, and he laughed awkwardly. "Yeah…I know."

My mind raced on. "Where does Hook stand?"

"He knows Stuart has used him for a much bigger plan," Paul replied. "And Hook now believes that Connor Lee, your book's Mr. Smee, didn't commit suicide."

"Tyler mentioned foul play on a wild night with The Monster. What did you hear?" Paul paused while reading a text. He pulled back with worry in his eyes, slid his phone into his back pocket, and ended the conversation. But was he worried for me or because of me?

"I must get going," he muttered nervously. "I'm glad I got to see you, Larry. I uh…hope I helped."

My head tilted. "You did," I said, wondering who texted him. "Thanks for the info, Paul."

After he left, I questioned Ashley about it. She thought that Paul's brother had become paranoid. He would share information, then want to take it back and hide. She swore that The Monster had that effect on people.

I tucked my phone in my back pocket and headed home, unable to stop thinking about what Paul shared. When I stopped at the Ocean Avenue light, I decided to call Ashley again and noticed her text. The light turned green. I turned onto A1A and read it: **The Monster's jet landed in Vero Beach last night. Today, he celebrated at the yacht club!**

I swerved back into my lane and read her follow-up: My friend's a server at the club. She thought it was strange that anyone would raise champagne flutes during a global pandemic, but they were partying on his new yacht like they were blue-collar workers who won the lottery!

I texted back: Who was with Stuart?

Caroline Haines was still by his side with two other couples.

How could Caroline be there after reading Carla's diary entry? I replied.

Caroline didn't believe it. But she did leave early, crying.

I arrived at our house fifteen minutes later. With a glance at the kitchen clock, I knew Allison would be back any minute, and I quickly scribbled in my notepad:

It feels like the truth of this is at the top of a mountain, and I am sinking in quicksand at the bottom.

I twitched as my phone rang. It was Ashley.

"Hey," I answered.

"The Yacht Club's manager confirmed that Stuart's party wasn't practicing social distancing as he preaches," she whispered. "It was hugs and kisses and caviar and champagne for six."

I stood, astonished.

"What were they celebrating?"

"If you believe Carla's whistleblowers, it would be the day the WHO declared a pandemic," she replied. "Carla wrote that one man dies, and another gets rich."

"This is insane," I said. "Absolutely insane."

"Sure is."

My phone pinged again.

"Okay. I'll call you later."

"Bye."

Click.

I rubbed my eyes and noticed that it was my daughter, Lauren: Hey, dad. I heard all gyms had to close and wanted to make sure you're okay.

I replied: I'm struggling a bit, but we need to catch up. I'm sorry I've been so busy.

Lauren responded: I understand. This is crazy. Jerry's home from college, so I'll bring him. We just have to find a restaurant that's still open. How does next week sound?

I enthusiastically typed: Great. I can't wait!

Five days later, the stay-at-home order was placed, and everyone remained in isolation. I felt like life was being sucked out of me. I needed sleep but opened my notepad to a new page, grabbed a pen, and wrote:

Cry it out and refocus. This is happening...

CHAPTER EIGHTEEN

MASKS, MAYHEM, AND A CALL FROM JOHN

APRIL 15, 2020

THE HOUSE

Allison stood on the other side of the family room, holding bags of groceries and a disposable mask. She glared at me as I read Ashley's latest text: **Stuart told Caroline that Carla became a writer because she feels the need to live a fictitious life that is more exciting than her own. Paul's brother believes Caroline knows the truth about The Monster. Anyway, I like Paul. I hope this stay-at-home order ends soon. Can you talk?**

I texted her back: **I'll call you later.**

Finally, I looked over at Allison. She grew stiff, waiting for me to say something. I wanted to hug her but felt like I'd be walking over broken glass to get to her. Instead, I waved, smiling awkwardly.

"Hey there...honey," I said. My tone was forcibly upbeat. "How was the grocery store?"

Her eyes narrowed at me. "Well, there's no toilet paper, and our neighbors are rinsing off their groceries in the driveway. Do you think we should start doing that?"

I released my breath in a heavy sigh. "No, I do not."

Allison was irritated by my cynical tone. "Please lighten up," she said, walking into the kitchen. "I bought us masks on Amazon. Did you hear we need to wear them at the grocery store?"

I crossed the room to the French doors and opened them wide. "Yes," I groaned. "I heard Dr. Folie changed his mind." I paused, turned back to her, and added, "Lately, America's doctor has been on TV more than The Monster."

Allison placed a Lean Cuisine in the microwave. "Do you want to have our groceries delivered?"

I considered that for several moments and said, "No, I'll wear the mask. Have you heard from Dr. Strange?"

Her mouth fell. She couldn't believe I had brought him up. "Larry...I don't want to fight."

"Neither do I. I'm concerned."

She took a calming breath. "I don't want to hear about Carla either."

"I heard a scientist working on the vaccine can prove this virus didn't come from any animal. He concluded it was engineered in a lab, proving Carla correct."

Allison gripped a can of peas. "Okay, but she also predicted this pandemic will last for years—Dr. Avery concluded that Carla's a promiscuous drama queen. He's been struggling badly with his depression, too," she said, turning to shelve the peas. "I only have a few minutes before my next Zoom class. Can you stay in the bedroom?"

I winced at her words and tried not to lose my temper. Everything grated on my nerves. I also tried not to watch her unpack the groceries because she'd leave every cabinet open, with something frozen, typically defrosting on the counter. Then I thought about Ashley's comment.

Love Allison exactly as she is.

When Allison mentioned her Zoom class again, I gripped my phone and crossed my arms. "How are these kids learning like this?"

"Most of them aren't," she said. "But I'm more worried about you." Her angry expression and tight tone of voice caused me to cringe.

My jaw dropped. "Me?"

"Yes, you must accept that it'll be May before The Gym can reopen."

I bowed my head and rubbed my thumb across my eyebrow. "Why are you saying that?"

"Dr. Folie has warned against re-opening too early." I didn't say anything, but I didn't have to. Allison continued, "He's predicting more outbreaks. So, please wear your mask."

My phone rang before we could get into the mask debate.

"I think this is one of my members," I said to Allison, hurrying outside. I answered right before it went to voicemail. "This is Larry."

A man's voice said, "Stuart Grossman is aware you're writing the story he can't have told."

"Who is this?"

"Call me John."

"How did you get my number?"

"Carla."

I hesitated, then asked, "What do you want?"

"My outlook on life has changed since the pandemic began. I know this sounds crazy, but you must expose the lies only as a fairy tale with a monster and a love that prevails against the greatest of odds."

I laughed. "I don't know who you are or why you're calling, but I honestly don't know what I'm writing."

He paused. "The temptation is powerful to close our eyes and wait for the worst to pass, but history tells us that in order for freedom to survive, it must be defended, and if the lies are to stop, they must be exposed."

"Is that a quote?"

"Yes, from Madeleine Albright. Any writer could see the corruption in this storyline. I realize this isn't easy to comprehend, but Carla told me a lot about you. She chose you because she claims you are the only one to write this dark fairy tale with a love that prevails when everything fails."

I took a shaky breath, recalling my dreams. I could only utter, "I met Carla once—"

"Carla's a hopeless romantic who believes that love conquers all. Maybe she sees you writing a story you might not see yet. Maybe she sees you writing a story you need to write."

"What do you mean?"

"This pandemic has not helped anyone's relationship."

"Carla should stick to researching viruses, not relationships."

"If you say so."

I paused to gather myself, but I couldn't. Instead, I cleared my throat. "So, what were you saying about Stuart—The Monster?"

"Stuart will try to control you. He has gone to great lengths to prevent this story from being told. I have friends at the firm. Once I confirm his plan, I'll be in touch. Until then, I suggest you keep taking notes. Carla feels it will all come together soon: She truly believes in your magical love."

I shook my head in confusion. "Hold on a second…John—"

The call ended.

What story am I meant to write?

Is this pandemic more than a mess of corruption?

I sighed, afflicted yet intrigued.

Does love really conquer all?

Will my relationship with Allison survive?

CHAPTER NINETEEN

NOW IS NOT A GOOD TIME

APRIL 16, 2020

THE HOUSE

I had another frustrating dream. After starting the coffee with a list of questions in my notepad and no answers, I tried to make sense of the inexplicable. I hadn't been this shaken since *The Show's* storyline when I lost my stellar career ten years ago. I wanted to believe everything would work out in the end, but I was consumed by the need to know how.

I sat at my notepad in the darkened kitchen and wrote:

I had another vivid dream. Carla insisted that all stories are love stories. Like her mysterious friend, she insisted I keep taking notes. I questioned her about the virus. She laughed. Then she repeated that line: All the best love stories have one thing in common. You must go against the odds to get there– "How's your fiancée?" Carla asked. I awoke in a panic. Was that a sign that Allison would get this virus? Is it that much worse than the flu?

Desperate for answers, I scrolled Carla's six-hundred-page book and stopped at an interview.

Chapter Fifty-Five – The Dr. Shawn Avery Interview – January 28, 2020:

Question: "Can you explain what an infectious disease doctor does?"

Dr. Avery: "There are dozens of infectious diseases, from the flu and pneumonia to the common cold. I am trained in clinical and laboratory skills to make the right diagnosis and organize the best treatment plans."

Question: "Why did you come forward, risking humiliation and ridicule to tell your side of this story?"

Dr. Avery: "I am speaking out because the world needs to know the truth."

Question: "Why do so many media outlets connect the origins of this virus to a wet market?"

Dr. Avery: "Because conflicted scientists are forced to lie when a cover-up goes all the way to the top."

Question: "Will this become a global pandemic?"

Dr. Avery: "Yes. I'm guessing the White House will order a stay-at-home order by April."

Question: "Do stay-at-home orders work?"

Dr. Avery: "Lengthy periods of isolation will cause mental health issues, increased suicide, alcohol dependency, depression, and will certainly have negative impacts on the economy—I can go on, but I'll sum it up. Stay-at-home orders for this virus do not make sense. Many of us have types of ACE2 that the virus spike cannot stick to. In other words, a healthy person might test positive but only have mild symptoms like a common cold."

Question: "If that's true, why doesn't the CDC talk about natural immunity?"

Dr. Avery: "Those promulgating vaccines will feel no need to address the science on this question; instead, they'll fall back on the CDC's recommendation that everyone gets vaccinated regardless of immunity status. The CDC will ignore the scientific evidence on this issue for many political reasons."

Question: "Why is this happening?"

Dr. Avery: "Money and greed. Stuart Grossman, Dr. Frank Folie, Big Pharma, and the vaccines. The Pharma-Folie alliance exercises dominion over global health policies. Vaccine mandates will be heard often in the coming year. Folie and Grossman will use their control of media outlets, science journals, government agencies, and global intelligence agencies to flood the public with fearful propaganda about the virus. They will muzzle debate and censor dissent even after the public realizes the truth. After the vaccine paydays, we'll say that it's truly criminal how leaders worldwide handled this virus.

I heard movement and looked up from the glow of my phone. Allison stood in the corner of the lanai with bloodshot eyes. She seemed tired, tense, and agitated. She knew what I was reading. Her eyes narrowed, still ice blue but now burning with fire. Finally, she said, "This story is consuming you, Larry."

My jaw tightened. "How are you feeling? I mean, do you have any symptoms?"

Something passed over Allison's face. I couldn't tell what. Then, she said, "No. I just want you back. I'm lonely. You just finished one book and are now writing and rewriting while obsessed with Carla's dark fairy tale."

There was so much to say, but neither of us knew where to go from there. I couldn't even disagree. I took another sip of coffee, thinking about what I had read, and mentioned Dr. Avery's interview. Allison only insisted that they'd stopped talking. She seemed adamant that debating cover-ups or conspiracy theories no longer interested her.

I smiled, equally frustrated and confused. "Okay, I don't want to fight."

She looked down at her feet as she stood in somewhat of an unsure posture. "Neither do I."

I tried to think of a response to change the subject, but a fit of anger flared within me, and I said, "The world is becoming a dangerous place. We have unpredictable leaders, an increasing concentration of wealth and power, and less and less transparency. Elites like The Monster want to gain control of everything. What's happening is extremely important—" she interrupted me.

"Larry, you're searching for answers you'll never get." We stared at each other as the tension grew thicker between us. After a moment, she walked back into the house. "So, please stop."

I drew in a calming breath. I couldn't stand the angst. I had no idea what was going on inside me. I couldn't deal with the excruciating feelings I had. There was no time for emotional adjustment. It was like

I put a Band-Aid on a bullet wound, waiting to bleed out. But I also knew Allison's depression had gotten the best of her.

I forced myself to check on her before her next Zoom class. Of course, I first had to confirm what day it was: The days were blurring together. I moved slowly into the family room and heard Allison in our bedroom. She was venting on the phone to her sister. I stood there for a moment, thinking about my kids and mother. I regretted not seeing them before the stay-at-home order. I wandered outside; I grabbed my Bose remote off the pool deck and hit my new pandemic playlist, hoping to relax.

Quickly I dozed off.

An hour later, my coffee was cold, and my eyes flickered open to "Cat's in the Cradle."

With watery eyes, I dialed my son. The cry helped, and I replayed the song when the call went to voicemail. I found that crying was the one thing that helped me deal with the isolation and this overwhelming rollercoaster of emotions that were fast consuming me.

Ping.

I blinked in a daze.

Did I hear something?

I yawned, glancing back into the house.

It was quiet.

Ping.

I had heard the sound a million times, yet it took me a moment to realize Ashley had texted me.

I wiped my eyes to read it: **My mom and dad are getting divorced. This stay-at-home order is killing them. I almost wish they would fight it out. But all they do is drink in excess at opposite ends of the house. Can you talk?**

I had enough problems being drowned away with wine and released an exasperated sigh. Then I typed: **Now is not a good time.**

CHAPTER TWENTY

A SPOONFUL OF SUGAR WITH A MEATBALL

APRIL 20, 2020

THE HOUSE

Fear changed everyone and everything, and yet, as always, life went on.

I took a sip of coffee, shocked by a late-night email from The Gym's landlord. They wanted my answer to a recent conference call that served as an ultimatum: Pay March and April's rent or vacate the space by June. And if I chose the latter, they would release me from the lease without owing them anything.

At first, I thought I couldn't do that. Over these years, a commitment made my decision-making easier. It removed any fear of missing out, knowing that I wanted to retire as the owner of The Gym. However, the outright rejection of alternatives wasn't as liberating amidst a lockdown. Sighing dramatically, I turned on the TV, nonetheless preparing how to tell Allison the news.

I took a deep breath and headed down the hall.

It was still dark when I entered our bedroom. Allison was sprawled across the middle of the bed. The comforter was on the floor beside her as the clock on the nightstand turned to 6:03. I decided not to wake her. Instead, I wandered back into the kitchen for more coffee. I could hear the news. A financial analyst predicted that this pandemic would plunge the global economy into the worst recession since World War II. I stood awkwardly, suppressing my yawns while counting the empty wine bottles on the counter.

I stopped at eight and began pacing the hallway.

A few minutes later, Allison's alarm sounded. I could choreograph the next few moments: She would hit snooze twice, then I'd have to remind her that the girls had to be picked up from their father's house at 8:00. It made no sense that we would share parenting time during a stay-at-home order, but not much of this was meant to make sense. Allison turned on the shower and summoned me to our bedroom. I walked in, and she looked at me with mad, feverish eyes.

"Do you miss the girls?" she asked, her lips curving into a hesitant smile. "It would be nice if you could get them for me."

I stood there motionless and silent, staring at the steam coming from the bathroom. "I have to talk to you."

The tight tone of my voice caused her smile to falter. "I need to shower if you don't want to go pick up the girls."

"Allison, it's about The Gym—"

"Wait," she said. "What day is it?"

"It's…like the end of April. Why?"

"I'm not joking," she said as she grabbed her phone off the nightstand. "If it's Monday, I have a Zoom class in two hours."

I couldn't help but joke about this maddening pandemic that had the world losing track of time, but I wanted to brighten her mood. "Well, you're a great teacher," I said enthusiastically. "Even on Zoom."

She shot me a look. "Half of these kids claim they can't hear me— and the other half sit in their pajamas eating cereal with their cameras facing a ceiling fan. I need you to get the girls for me—"

"Okay," I said, hurrying out of the bedroom. "We can talk later."

I snatched my keys off the kitchen counter and quietly closed the front door.

Later that day, after Allison's Zoom classes, I approached her in the kitchen to tell her the news. She placed a half-empty bottle of wine down with a thud and stuck a tiny spoon in a pan of meatballs while singing "A Spoonful of Sugar" in a rather impressive Julie Andrews voice. "Just a spoonful of sugar helps the medicine go down, the medicine go down—medicine go down—" she looked up at me "— what?" The meatball had fallen off the tiny spoon, hit her knee, and rolled across the Kitchen. I stared at her, open-mouthed. "What's wrong?" she asked.

"Oh, um…." I paused as her gaze shifted back to the pan. "I think you need a bigger spoon."

Her expression made it clear that she was clueless about what had happened. "What?"

I shook my head. "The meatball hit your knee and rolled across the floor."

"What are you talking about?"

"The sauce on your knee," I said, pointing to it. "It hit your knee and rolled over there."

She blinked downward and then to the trail of sauce. "No, Josie dropped that when she took her plate into her room." Allison put the tiny spoon in the pan and took another sip of wine. "I'll talk to her," she added. "Just stop being so intense. Josie's only a little girl." I opened my mouth and closed it. Then Allison finished with: "A spoonful of sugar helps the medicine go down — in the most delightful way!"

This is a slapstick comedy.

Since I poured myself a huge glass of wine, I couldn't lecture Allison about the empties on the counter, so I walked outside for some fresh air instead.

A few hours later, around 6:00, I was still attempting to explain the landlord dilemma to Allison. I peeked into the family room and noticed her sitting on her yoga mat in the Lotus position, binge-watching *The Golden Girls* reruns. I took careful steps back to the kitchen and refilled my wine glass. All the cabinets were open, her frying pan still had meatballs, and the empty wine bottles seemed to be multiplying on the counter.

"So, what're the benefits of drunk yoga?" I asked her, heading into the family room with a raised wine glass. "If you have an extra mat, I'd like to join you."

Allison started to say something and then seemed to think better of it. "First, you need to trust the science. I watched an enlightening interview with Dr. Folie and Stuart Grossman today."

I spilled wine on my T-shirt. "Yes, I didn't want to interrupt that," I said, forcing myself to nod. "But I do need to talk to you."

She continued, "Don't be sarcastic, Larry. Just trust the science."

I took a slow, calming breath. "Those men are manipulating data. It's not science, Allison—"

"Stop preaching Carla's words."

I sighed, then stiffened. "The Gym's landlord called with a deal to let me out of the lease."

She swayed on her mat, taken aback. "Wait. What do you mean?"

"He said I wouldn't have to pay March or April's rent if I'm out by June—"

She gasped, "Out by June?"

"Yes. It would release me from the remaining six months of the lease." My voice cracked as I said it, and I felt like crying—or maybe laughing. I took a long sip of wine and tried to get a hold of myself.

"What if you file for that virus-relief loan?" she asked anxiously.

I answered her question with another question. "What if this virus has spooked too many members into buying Pelotons?"

Allison's face took on that sad, semi-judgmental look that I hated. "I was worried about this. How are you going to get another job? What are you going to do?"

I tried to put my indecision into words. I believed there had to be something I could do to save The Gym, but this wasn't my last storyline. This was a pandemic. I wasn't even sure when I could reopen. "I'm going to tell them I won't be able to decide until the state reopens," I finally said. "But let's talk about it in the morning."

She breathed out. "I can't believe this—"

"We should talk in the morning."

Allison looked scared. "No."

My heart was too heavy to continue.

"Yes, it's best," I insisted. "With your Zoom classes and cooking dinner…at three in the afternoon…during that wine tasting." I paused and enthusiastically added, "And your singing! I love your voice. A Spoonful of Sugar. That was beautiful, but you must be exhausted."

She blinked, seemingly desperate to focus on anything but the reality of this moment. "Aw," she smiled at me, "do you really think I have a beautiful voice?"

I smiled back at her. "I do."

CHAPTER TWENTY-ONE

ARE WE GOING TO SURVIVE THIS?

MAY 4, 2020

THE HOUSE

It was the first Monday in May.

With news of the state reopening, I was anxious to hear back from Carla's mysterious friend, John. I was also jittery about calling the landlord with my decision. When it rang a fourth time, my heart pounded as I prepared to leave a voicemail.

But then, "Good morning, this is Mike."

"Mike, it's Larry…from The Gym," I replied, irritated that he pretended he didn't know.

He hesitated. "What is your decision?"

"I'm staying," I said emphatically. "I love that gym."

"Larry, unemployment rates are climbing. The worst rate since the Great Depression."

"Mike, we both know that exaggerated number includes temporary layoffs."

"Define temporary," he said. "These are unprecedented times."

"I must make…." my voice cracked. "I must make this work."

"People are driving around alone in their cars with masks on. No one is planning to return to any fitness centers."

The jolt I felt almost caused me to drop my phone.

He continued, "We lowered your rent rate for years, and we must raise it back at the end of your lease."

I struggled for a breath. "How can you do this now?" I asked, fuming. "I have spent a fortune—"

"Larry if you had the financial backing to wait this out, I would advise you to do so. But you don't. Besides, no one could've predicted this pandemic."

I swallowed hard. "I know a few who had—"

"Look at your options and call me next week. I must take this call—"
Click.

They wanted me out, plain and simple. I collapsed on the family room couch.

This decision consumed my days, and now, after making it, I had to reevaluate it again. I took a slow breath and turned up the news. A reporter suggested that the President's absurd remark that we treat the virus by injecting disinfectant, like bleach, into the body was a direct jab at Dr. Folie. The two men despised each other as Folie flip-flopped on various virus measures and recommendations. 'Dr. Folie has changed positions, proving his stances are flawed on issues ranging from mask-wearing to the severity of the virus,' the reporter stated. 'From asymptomatic spreading to effective treatments for patients— Folie has misled the public. We need oversight into a position that has abused its power and has been responsible for many failures during this lockdown—one that will ruin small businesses.'

In contrast, big businesses remained open and were doing quite well. Putting more power into the hands of big companies was suitable for politicians; it was easier to collude with thousands of big companies than tens of millions of smaller ones. But this was in no way good for the economy, and pretending otherwise was a dangerous farce. I turned off the news. As far as I could see, the fearful public was convinced the only way out of this mess was through a vaccine. And many of them were prepared to wear two masks while driving alone in their cars while waiting for it.

I leaned back and dozed off.

Two hours later, Allison whispered, "Larry…." she shook my arm. "You fell asleep."

My eyes flickered open. "Oh hey…."

Allison hurried through her to-do list: "I dropped the girls back off at their father's, stopped by Wal-Mart for a few things, bought some more masks at CVS, and picked up a bottle of Josh cabernet so we can toast your book release."

I blinked at her. "That's next month."

"Oh…I guess I'll have to psych myself up all over again."

I sat up. "What does that mean?"

"I was no perfect pixie when we lived that storyline out, but you still fell in love with me."

I rubbed my face. "I'm not following."

"You've changed, Larry. I know it's easy to blame my depression and drinking, but you have changed and refuse to see it."

"No–I'm just trying to understand."

"Never mind. Just keep flying off to your sacred Never Land." Allison was on the verge of tears.

A wave of emotion swept over me, and I couldn't speak. I needed a moment I didn't have. I reached out my hand and gently touched the side of her face. She pulled away, poured a glass of wine, and disappeared into our bedroom. I followed her, exhausted and angry. When I got to the door, I only had one question.

I knocked softly.

"Allison, are we going to survive this?"

"I don't know."

How does anyone survive something like this?

CHAPTER TWENTY-TWO

THE RE-OPENING

MAY 18, 2020

THE GYM

For two weeks, I rode on an emotional pendulum that swung between hope and despair.

Now, amidst my relationship drama, I had the daunting challenge of reopening a fitness center during a time of tumult. I pulled into The Gym's eerily quiet parking lot, hopped out of my car, and inhaled the intoxicating smell of the ocean. I tilted my head back for some vitamin D and winced when an angry voice startled me.

"Put on your mask!"

I turned and squinted at an older lady three rows over. "I'm sorry. I didn't see you...over there."

She took hold of her hatchback, wearing rubber gloves, and slammed it on a bundle of toilet paper. "What did you say?"

"I hope you have a good day!"

I sighed, snatched my mask off the passenger seat, and stomped to my bench. I sat down, baffled by another person alone in their car wearing a mask, and stood back up. It occurred to me how much I missed the smiling faces of the cyclists and the shout-outs from the skateboarders. The absence of laughter was disheartening. I would never have thought such a beautiful day could feel so dreary. It was a direct reminder of my dreaded call with the landlord. My mind reeled while approaching the dark fitness center. I wiped the cobwebs off the door, closed my eyes, and tried to clear my mind.

A moment later, I spun to a honking horn. My long-lost smile hid behind my mask as I waved, relieved to see Aurora pull up in her minivan. Her lovely, maskless face glowed as she leaned out of her window. "Hey, boss!"

"You can't tell," I said, pointing to my mask. "But I'm so happy to see you."

Aurora laughed and got out of her van. "I am so happy to see you. Please open our gym."

Her words were comforting. For the moment, I felt better. But as we chatted, Aurora mentioned seeing Caroline crying at the beach. I pondered that and was irately intrigued. I tried to change the subject, but then I circled back. "So, was Caroline alone?"

"Yes, the beach was empty," Aurora replied solemnly, shifting her gaze around the parking lot. "Like this plaza."

"When was this?"

"This morning, when I took Zak surfing. We walked right by her sobbing in a BMW under the tall palm at Coconut Point Park," she said, half smiling. "So, did you ever find out if Caroline is a villain?"

I shook my head, wondering if it was best that Aurora's question went unanswered. I wanted to tell her about Carla's diary entry, my landlord dilemma, and the mysterious call from John. I decided to hold off on the tragicomedy that was my life, and instead, I forced a smile. "I'm only focused on The Gym. Please spread the word that we will officially reopen tomorrow."

"Yes!" she shouted, with an enthusiastic high five. "You bet I will."

In the corner of my eye, I noticed a car pass us and stop. The driver opened their window. "The CDC has mandated masks and social distancing for a reason," the lady yelled and sped off.

I filled the stunned silence. "At least she wasn't wearing one alone in her car. It was almost refreshing to see her scowling face."

Aurora grinned, shaking her head. "I can't wait to get back to normal," she said. "I'll come in tomorrow when you're open." She paused and gestured to my bench. "To see you sitting on that bench made my day. I'll see you tomorrow."

I nodded, uncharacteristically speechless.

With a tight grip on the fitness center's key, I opened the door and struggled to breathe. It was musty and hot. I wiped my forehead and hurried to the yoga studio thermostat. It was set to 80 but read 86. I rushed to the next—the same thing. I ripped off my mask and ran out the back door. The large puddle indicated that only one unit had been running nonstop to overcompensate for the others that weren't.

I felt lightheaded and knelt. Then a text flashed up: Larry, Ralph Stein here. I left two voicemails at The Gym but haven't heard back from you. Please suspend my membership. They are predicting this to get worse before it gets better. Stay safe.

I stood up and wiped more sweat beads from my forehead. After making my way into the office, I hit the flashing voicemail button:

Hi Larry. It's Claire Smith. I preordered your book but need to cancel my membership. Your book should be here in a couple of weeks. I'll call you back after I read it. Stay home. Stay safe, dear.

Beep.

Hi, Larry! It's Gloria. My doctor won't allow me to return to The Gym. We don't know how it will survive. I'll call you again in June when I get your book. I can't wait to read it. Okay, bye.

Beep.

Larry, it's Margie Madison. Please cancel my membership. I wish we didn't have that lunatic Governor opening the state early. Dr. Folie says it's not safe to be in any public setting. Call me.

That was the last voicemail I could tolerate.

I took a moment to think things through and alter my game plan. I mentally noted the older members who couldn't come back and started dialing the younger ones who could. Almost all of them planned on returning but not during a hot Florida summer without cool air. I called Ashley for some even younger options.

I began pacing as it rang.

On the fourth ring, she answered, breathing heavily. "H-e-y…."

"Would your friends lift in a gym without air conditioning?"

I heard a slight moan. And then a young man's voice whispered, "Fuck…hang up—"

Ashley giggled. "Sorry…yeah…sure." —another moan— "we love sweating…."

"Oh, wow," I said, rolling my eyes. "Say hi to Paul and call me later—"

Click.

My heart sank a little as I looked around. I turned on all the TVs to ensure they still worked and noticed a reporter in front of men in hazmat suits moving body bags out of a hospital. I turned up the volume. 'Dr. Folie has warned against re-opening too soon and predicts more outbreaks in light of rolling back physical distancing protocols,' the reporter said. I shook my head and wandered away. I stared out into the deserted parking lot, sifting slowly in my mind through bad option after bad option. Every HVAC company ran weeks behind, while most couldn't even get any parts. A voice startled me.

"Hey, Larry, can you send me a chapter of the new book?"

I spun around to a young surfer who was a member when I took over The Gym. I hadn't seen him in a few years and couldn't recall his name. I continued to look directly at him. "*The Gym* will be out the first week of June."

"Ashley sent me that story," he replied, nodding with a thumbs up. "How about the one Carla Kimbrel has you writing?"

I regarded him for a silent moment, although not surprised. "What do you know about that?" I asked, intrigued.

"We all embark on a journey of love. You found it in the last book. But now you must save it during a global pandemic with an evil monster."

I chuckled at how bizarre that sounded and said, "Are you high?"

He grinned. "A little."

"So, how do you know Carla?"

"From the firm," he said, giggling. "I was on Sharky's sales team. I saw you the night you wrote about in *The Gym*—the night you met Sharky." He glanced at all the memories on the walls. "I miss those days. Before The Monster ruined everything, Carla joined the firm. She was a hot blonde—a writer. Romance stories and shit…she loved to live life and laugh. Anyway, I was heading to get a sub next door when I saw your doors open." He started walking out, stopped, and turned to me. "I can get Carla's diary entries if it would help inspire your new story."

My eyes locked with his again. "How do you have those?" I asked a little bit too desperately.

"We printed out her emails when she worked at the firm. They were always entertaining."

I nodded. "Yes, I'd be interested. Thank you."

"You bet, Pan Man. Stay focused on the stories with the guy trying to keep it together while falling apart." He grinned. "We relate to you. It's life."

I sat at the desk and opened my notepad.

Fifteen minutes went by before I even looked up. I studied the five months of notes I had taken and saw notifications on my phone screen. "Shit," I said aloud. I had two missed calls from Allison, a text from Ashley, and three more member cancellations.

How did I miss these?

I squeezed my eyes shut and swallowed the lump in my throat.

What is wrong with me?

I was instantly irritable and pushed my notepad away as anger clouded my judgment. Fear had caused me to boil over.

Fuck!

I paced The Gym, unable to control the dark thoughts that consumed me.

Breathe.

I'm going to lose The Gym.

Calm down!

I'm going to lose Allison.

Calm down!

There's no love or enchantment in this maddening story.

CALM DOWN!

My muscles tensed. I only felt fear and defensiveness. Quickly, the hot fitness center became intolerable. I closed The Gym and staggered into the grocery store to pick up some essentials. I grabbed a few bottles of water and flinched.

"You came in the wrong way!" an employee snapped. "Look at the arrows on the floor."

What the fuck?!

I repositioned the bottles in my arms. "Come on. There's no one here—"

"Sir, it doesn't matter," he said, carefully adhering to Dr. Folie's social distancing protocol. "You must follow the arrows."

"The arrows?" I said, deliberately stepping forward to see if he'd fall back. And he did so as if I were pointing a gun at him. "Hey, relax. I don't want to break any of Dr. Folie's rules. I just want to understand."

He adjusted his mask with his rubber gloves. "Sir, this is a deadly virus."

"Oh, yes, I've heard that," I said sarcastically. As the young man took another step back, I drew in a breath and added, "So, which way was I supposed to come in?"

"You should've gone up that aisle and come back down this one." I sighed heavily, apologized, and asked him which way I should go to pay. He pointed the wrong way. "Follow those arrows and stop at the red tape." I blinked and was utterly disoriented. He continued, "When you get there, wait for me. I'll wave you to a register when it is safe."

When it's safe?

I shook my head, then I nodded once and hurried along.

Ten minutes later, Allison called. I answered like Eeyore, "Heello."

She asked me where I was, but I could tell something was wrong. I lowered the car's air conditioning and told her I was on my way home. She insisted that we needed to talk. I gripped the steering wheel, took a breath, and agreed.

She continued, "The real world isn't Never Land. I can't live up to your unrealistic expectations."

I exhaled what felt like every breath I'd been holding around her lately. "Allison, on second thought, I need to be home to have this conversation."

"No, this pandemic has been a living hell for everyone, but I choose to move on—"

Anger crept into my voice. "How do you move on with no end in sight?"

It sounded like she started to cry. Then, "How's The Gym?"

"It's terrible…there's no air."

"What?"

"Our air conditioning died."

"Didn't you just replace those units?"

"Three years ago," I said and sighed. "Nothing lasts in the salt air."

"What members are coming back?"

I tightened my grip on the steering wheel and mumbled, "Not nearly enough."

I heard a door slam on her end of the phone.

"I've decided we need some space." She paused briefly and added, "I'm leaving the house now."

I stopped short, nearly hitting the car in front of me. "What?"

"I must figure out what's best for my girls and me."

Her words knocked the breath from me. My screen went dark.

In shock, I muttered, "Allison…."

The call ended.

CHAPTER TWENTY-THREE

IT'S A WILD WORLD

MAY 19, 2020

THE HOUSE

It was twenty-four hours since Allison walked out of the house and twenty-four hours since I'd heard from her. My whole world came crashing down, yet I had a small hint of strength.

Since nothing made sense, I followed my heart with an overwhelming urge to scroll through our pictures. With each one, I could not explain how her blue eyes and bright smile made my heart skip a beat. Then, I paused when I came to one of our last photos together. A server took it at The Fish House just before Christmas. Allison looked flustered.

As I stared at the photo, I recalled why my fiancée had been distracted. She had received a text at the table from Dr. Avery. It was the first time I'd heard his name. But that wasn't the only reason I let this night slip from my memory. Allison's demeanor darkened when I received a call from my publisher. She also thought that our fairy tale had changed me. In her mind, I'd lost sight of the man who had tripped and fallen, gotten up, and was led to her, a better person.

My mind recalled that December night in 2019. I had blocked out her concerns that I expected to live out an unrealistic version of my book's happily ever after.

At that moment, I could see her face as she stared at me across our favorite table by the river. I heard Allison's voice:

"Larry, there will never be perfect bliss in an imperfect world. We are all broken."

Is she being overly sensitive?

I looked at her for a moment, unsure how to take her words. Life was good. We worked hard to get to this point. I felt she should've been more appreciative of where we were. Somehow, I swallowed my disappointment. I opened my mouth to apologize but got cut off by a text she had received.

The ping echoed eerily.

Curiosity flashed in her eyes. Something had changed, and I couldn't tell if it was good or bad. Now, I'm annoyed at how fickle my feelings could be.

"Who is that?" I asked, glaring at her.

She didn't answer right away. Almost as if she had to give the question some thought. "Oh, it's a doctor. A friend. I knew him before I met you."

My heart began to beat faster. "What's his name?"

"Shawn Avery," Allison replied, reading his text. "Anyway, life will get ugly again, Larry. Beware."

"Well, this was fun. Awkward reality checks and ex-boyfriends. Check, please."

A hint of a smile played at the edges of her mouth. For a moment, she looked more relaxed. Then, she tried to lighten the mood. "Oh, Peter, this wild world isn't all made of pixie dust, dear!"

I shrugged sullenly when her doctor friend sent a follow-up text, and the evening ended abruptly.

After reliving that night, I was done looking at our pictures. I sat at the kitchen table, opened my notepad, and wrote:

We are all broken. That's how the light gets in–Ernest Hemingway.

On the outside, our lives looked blissful. And much of it was. But that was the problem. After writing The Gym, I was only focused on the happily-ever-after. I had taken Allison for granted, and she had started communicating with Dr. Avery. Our relationship had lost a little trust, stability, and compassion right before this wild world spun into a global pandemic.

I blinked back my watery eyes, missing everything that drove me crazy during the stay-at-home order: The lights she'd leave on, the cabinets she'd leave open, the meals left on the stove, her Hallmark channel marathons, her clothes drying from every door frame in the house—everything.

I paced the hallway and heard her voice—Allison frantically yelling for me to find her phone again. I smiled and noticed a box full of her wedding magazines. For the past year, they had been scattered around the house. I remembered the last time she held one, close to her heart and hopeful for a summer wedding. It was the same day I told her about Carla's call.

I sighed, shaking my head.

Then my phone pinged.

I lunged for it, hoping it was Allison. But it was Ashley: Don't yell at me, but I haven't opened The Gym yet! My bestie's parents, who were happily married before the lockdown, are now getting a divorce. Her mother suffers from depression too. It's been bad. Anyway, I promised to spend some time with her, so I'm picking her up on the way. We'll be at The Gym after a Starbucks run if anyone calls you.

With that came another thought. After making my way back to my notepad, I continued writing:

No matter how blissfully content you were in your relationship before March 2020, there is no denying that the pandemic tore us out of our comfort zones and faced us to face a scary, new reality with no return to normalcy in sight....
It's time to adjust.

I placed the pen down. I couldn't deny that my comfort zone had become a twisted version of the fairy tale I had written. I shivered thinking about it. Suddenly, I viewed Carla differently: Was her interview some strange twist of fate? Did she come into my life to shake me out of this unrealistic dream state I had been drifting through?

Appreciation and gratitude.

Again, I picked up my pen, tapped it on the pad, thinking, and added:

Life happens for us, not to us.

This was an awakening of sorts. I texted Allison that I needed to talk to her.

It was early that evening when she replied: Since the day we met, you had this way of making this wild world feel like something else. For a couple of years, it was magical. But lately, it's been different. You have had no patience for me while being obsessed with Carla's story because it forced you out of the fantasy you were so content living. Adding your imaginary backdrop to your books is one thing, but believing you can live it out in this wild world is another. I'm staying with my parent's until I know what's best for my girls and me. I hope you respect my wishes if I want to start something new.

I placed my phone down, shaking.

After the initial shock of her message, I released my breath as a feeling of disappointment washed through me. I wanted to tell her that I agreed with her: Wholeheartedly.

How could I allow this to happen?

I went to call her, but I had to wipe the tears streaming down my face. I put my phone down again and tried to calm down.

After pouring a glass of wine, I walked over to my notepad. Still shaking, I spilled a few drops on a page as I hovered over it, deep in thought.

And then, I wrote my last line of the evening:

To love in this wild world is the greatest adventure of all.

I added a song to my pandemic playlist and headed down to the fire pit with my Bose remote. As the summer sun faded beyond our lush landscaping, I took a sip of wine and turned up Cat Stevens' "Wild World."

La-la-la-la-la-la-la-la-la-la

Now that I've lost everything to you

You say you wanna start something new

And it's breakin' my heart you're leavin'

Baby, I'm grievin'

But if you wanna leave, take good care

Hope you have a lot of nice things to wear

But then a lot of nice things turn bad out there

Oh, baby, baby, it's a wild world....

CHAPTER TWENTY-FOUR

SOCIAL UNREST

MAY 30, 2020

THE GYM

The pandemic began revealing the social cracks in our country.

It was a sweltering Saturday. I repeatedly wiped my forehead while on hold with another HVAC company. As the minutes ticked away, I sank into the office chair with the gym's landline pressed to my ear and noticed Ashley coming in fast.

I tensed, knowing too well what was coming.

"Larry, it's so fucking hot in here," she said, snatching a TV remote off the desk. "Can I grab more Evian for my friends?"

"Hold on, Ashley," I groaned. "Half of them haven't paid for the day." I paused and sighed. "But...go ahead."

"Thanks. How are things with your Tink?"

A loud moan was my answer.

I expected her follow-up, but none came.

When I spun the chair, Ashley raised the volume on the TVs above the spin bikes. Seconds later, an empty Evian bottle hit a TV as one of her friends yelled: "If you think our mask makes it hard to breathe, imagine being black in America!"

Then another shouted, "This is bullshit!"

"The police system doesn't work!" a third added.

I gripped the outdated phone as more of Ashley's possie strode through the open doors to join the protest. My head swiveled, almost back to front, like an owl.

"Ashley," I snapped. "I'm on the phone—"

Ashley didn't hear me as the shout-outs continued.

"Silence is violence!"

"Black Lives Matter!"

The young women were referring to an ongoing wave of civil unrest in the U.S. triggered by the murder of George Floyd, a black man, during his arrest by Minneapolis police officers just days before. Thousands took to the streets to protest anti-black racism in support of the Black Lives Matter movement.

I hurried outside.

Finally, a voice answered: "Sir, are you still there?"

"Yes, I'm still here!" I said hysterically. "I need someone to come out and fix my air."

"I'm sorry, sir, we can't get the parts for commercial units because of the pandemic."

"Can you recommend another company?" The call went dead. "Hello—" I shook the phone, and the battery flew out. "—shit!"

Aurora walked up. "Can you believe all this mayhem?"

"No," I said, collapsing on my bench. "This country is boiling over."

Aurora glanced at Ashley's friends and lowered her voice. "The media's making everyone nuts."

I didn't answer, mostly because I was afraid that if I had, my anger would show. Instead, I stood up and smiled, which couldn't hide how tired and drained I was. Aurora's presence was a huge help. Honestly, I didn't know how I would have made it through these past couple of weeks without her. Allison had taken time to figure out her future, and Aurora stepped in as my only prudent encouragement. She spent endless hours with me and always pointed out how far the fitness center had come. Aurora countered my mounting issues with a memory that tickled her while constantly reminding me of all the members who had fond memories of The Gym. As we returned to the office, Aurora recommended a Facebook donation page. Ashley eavesdropped ecstatically and agreed to set it up.

I peeked over her shoulder and heard thunder in the distance.

My nerves stretched thin.

My heart raced.

"Is it live yet?"

"You're an impatient little boy, Peter!" Ashley said, shaking her head. "Give me ten minutes."

The sea breeze kicked up, and I shut the doors to The Gym as the summer sky gave up all traces of blue. It had been nearly two weeks since Allison's text, but I retreated to the yoga studio with her on my mind. Lighting flashed in the window as my heart ached. I closed my eyes, unsure how to get a handle on myself and how to quiet my brain. For the next fifteen minutes, I focused on weathering this financial emergency. That didn't help. My options were minimal, the cancellations were plentiful, and most of Ashely's friends owed me more than they had paid.

With a sigh, I moved back into the office, hopeful that this donation page would provide a glimmer of hope. "Okay, I'm back," I said, trying to sound optimistic. "Are we ready?"

Ashley crossed her fingers. "Three – two – YES!"

A few minutes later, the first donation flashed up—seconds after that, the next.

Within twenty minutes, we had nearly a thousand dollars from a wide range of members. Although that amount didn't cover much, I sighed, relieved, thinking we might have a chance. I called Allison to share the news, but it went to her voicemail. I didn't leave a message. The donations energized me, but I was torn. I gripped my phone, knowing I shouldn't text my fiancée, but I did: **I miss you. I miss my best friend.**

Aurora moved toward me. "This is great news, boss!"

The smile she gave me made me want to cry.

An hour later, I did.

As the summer storms rolled through, Ashley rechecked the page. The rain poured down, and the lights flickered. She mumbled incoherently as if she was trying to hide her words. My stomach twisted even more.

The anticipation!

Finally, she shifted her weight to face me. "Is it possible the amount decreased?"

Aurora waved off the idea. "No. What's the problem?"

"A bunch of troubling comments," Ashley replied, pointing to the screen.

I leaned forward to read one: 'Your greed will kill our community!'

My eyes flickered through the next five:

'EVERYTHING MUST REMAIN CLOSED!'

'Put the weights down and MASK UP!'

'You're spreading the deadliest disease known to humanity!'

'Kill yourself, not us!'

'The vaccines won't save us if you kill us first!'

Aurora nudged me. "I don't recognize any of these names," she said. She was agitated, which was very rare for her. "Something's wrong."

Ashley shrugged with a look of confusion. "Yeah, and most of them are wearing masks…what the…." her voice trailed off.

I was devastated.

"Delete the page…." I muttered, struggling for a breath.

An awkward silence was broken by one of Ashley's friends. "Hey, it's Stuart Grossman."

We turned to the TVs.

The local news was interviewing The Monster. I shook my head, listening to him as he spoke through his fancy mask. Today, he acted as if he cared about a small mom-and-pop restaurant. 'It brings me great joy to help this family during such challenging times,' he said, handing them a check.

It has been said that "Money is Power," and today, that seemed more accurate than ever. As Americans suffered massive unemployment and ravages of the pandemic, The Monster and his lobbyists sought subsidies for the rich and corporations while demanding an end to supplemental assistance for ordinary working people. It was corruption at its worst. And undermined our democracy, yet the crowd cheered him on.

The charismatic tech titan moved forward, waving at the masked crowd as they held up their phones to take his picture. Amidst this global commotion, The Monster took advantage of the chaos to impose even more control over another vulnerable small business owner.

I swallowed hard, wishing I could speak with Carla.

Then I flinched as my phone rang. Allison was calling me back.

I took a breath and answered, "Hey."

"Hey," she said tiredly. "Please don't text me for a while."

"Okay," I said, stunned. "If that's what you want." I cringed as the words left my mouth. I wanted to scream out that I loved her, but I let the call end.

I walked outside.

Aurora followed. "Are you okay?"

I pressed my hand against my forehead, hoping to relieve the pain. "No. I feel like I'm fighting a battle that doesn't want to be won. I don't know. I'm beyond tired and have cried a river."

She frowned. "A true relationship has tears." Lighting lit up the darkened space. "That was a sign. I read the last page of your notepad. You're getting it." I found the strength to smile, but I couldn't answer. Another wave of dizziness caused me to sit on my bench cautiously. I folded my arms across my chest, taking in slow breaths. Stress: I had it tenfold. Thoughts: I should've had some of those, but I couldn't find one. Aurora sat beside me with impeccable timing and a reassuring pat on my knee. "Do you realize how many members call your love with Allison magical?"

I sighed exhaustedly, thinking about the call. "I wish I could see it as I used to."

Aurora smiled, shaking her head. "Your love is like the wind, you can't always see it, but everyone can feel it."

CHAPTER TWENTY-FIVE

THE OUT

MAY 31, 2020

THE GYM

The following morning, I received another call from John.

Finally, Carla's mysterious friend confirmed Stuart's plan. The tech titan devised a strategy to entice me to stop writing the story he repeatedly buried. Interestingly, John's snitch at the firm copied emails between The Monster and the fitness center's leasing group. The ugly truth came soon enough. I listened intently as John confirmed that Stuart had sent the first email shortly after Caroline's scripted visit.

I paced the yoga studio, insisting that I read them. As John explained that Stuart had strong ties to the leasing group, pictures of the emails flashed on my screen. The first proved what I suddenly feared: The Monster had influenced them to push me out. I returned to the fan in my office, breathing heavily and sweating. I took a sip of water and read each email, taken aback. Until then, I hadn't understood how losing The Gym could prevent me from writing this story. As John rambled on about Stuart's political aspirations, I interrupted him.

"This makes no sense. If I lose The Gym, I'll write this story just to burn his ass!"

"Part of his plan is saving your fitness center."

Only sheer willpower kept me from gasping. "What?"

"He recently saved a local restaurant. The owner's daughter is a journalist who withdrew a scathing article about Stuart in exchange for his large donation."

"I saw that," I admitted. "On the news."

For the next few minutes, John explained that Stuart planned on taking the same approach for The Gym while using the release of my novel as a PR event for himself. Stuart would appear to be a savior: The community would embrace him, and his donation would prevent me from writing the truth about him. I pressed the phone to my ear, and my heart was beating furiously at the sound of John's voice. I collapsed in the office chair and wiped the sweat off my forehead as John's message wound down with, "Stuart knows you're desperate. He also knows your novel is being released next week. His staff will reach out to you to sell you this plan."

"What's his plan?"

"You can take his money and pretend he's a savior or lose your gym and write the wrong story."

John's certainty was disarming yet astonishing. I was so lost in thought that I wasn't sure if I wanted to scream or cry. Instead, I took a breath, wondering who this guy really was. But that didn't help. More words were pressing the inside of my throat, wanting to release.

"I thought you wanted me to tell this story?"

"Carla already wrote that one."

"It's the same story."

"It will be if you're controlled by your angst. Ashley sent Carla your latest notes. You're getting it. You nailed The Monster and mayhem. Now focus on your magical love." He took a breath and released it. "A happily ever after in this book will not come easy. However, Carla now believes you will eventually turn this into a much-needed story of hope. I trust she is correct. Good luck, Larry."

Click.

Indeed, this was troublesome and enlightening.

I scribbled in my notepad:

The Monster, Mayhem, & Magical Love!

The Gym seemed to close around me; it was stifling, warm, and airless. Frowning, I rose from the chair, picked up the fan, and held it in front of my face. My eyes fluttered closed. Then I heard Ashley's voice.

"I finally got a job."

My eyes flew open as she rushed into the office. I placed the fan on the desk. "Where?"

We both plopped down beside each other.

She grinned eerily. "On Stuart's yacht." She saw the shock in my eyes and froze.

At that moment, I knew that Stuart had manipulated everyone yet again. I tried not to let the panic overwhelm me. I asked her how that could've happened as calmly as I could. She brought up her dad. I never knew the surgeon played golf with Stuart. She spoke about her father playing in his charity events. But it didn't end there. The Monster had furnished expensive ski vacations to Vail for him. Ashley stood up, distraught. "My dad makes a lot of money. Why would he take anything from Stuart?" She began pacing.

I sighed. "I need to tell you something."

She had looked away then, and her face puckered into a frown. "You can't talk me out of this."

We held each other's gaze.

"It's no coincidence that The Monster showed up at your house."

"I know," she said, nodding. "My dad insists that Stuart has much influence over many careers. He's been acting so weird since my parents announced that they were getting a divorce. I can't take it." I shook my head in silence and wanted to tell her about John. Ashley always possessed an uncanny ability to read me. And with a deep breath, she beat me to it. "John is Paul's brother." I looked up sharply. Her lips flattened as she anxiously brushed something off her shorts. "He wants to help," she insisted. "His real name is Chad."

I closed my eyes for a moment because I had to.

Swaying in the chair, I said, "I didn't think we needed a Deep Throat."

Her head tilted, confused. "Deep Throat?"

"A pseudonym given to the secret informant of Watergate…never mind, go on."

Twenty minutes later, she told me everything. John, who was Chad, was close friends with Carla. This coordinated effort to have me write this story now had Ashley nervous for me. Her eyebrows narrowed together as everything played out in her mind.

"We know that Stuart has had people murdered. That's why my dad's a wreck. At least this plan would keep everyone alive." She leveled a gaze at me. "If you take his money, you get back your fiancée and fitness center. Just take his money. Please, Larry!"

"The Monster's money isn't an option."

She rolled her big brown eyes. "I wanted you to write this story, but now it's way too dangerous. It's not just Stuart. Those corrupt bastards will kill you, Larry."

My gaze slowly shifted to all the pictures around The Gym. Most of the people in the photos were from my last storyline. I closed my mind to the memories.

"I must talk to Allison."

Ashley drew in a breath. "You guys aren't speaking right now." She wanted me to look at her, but I couldn't. She grabbed her purse and left, frustrated by my indecision about what she thought was an obvious out.

A wave of regret passed through me. I pushed myself out of the office chair and wandered to the TVs. America's doctor spoke about more outbreaks and the vaccines. I tried desperately to pull myself together.

Then a ping sounded on my phone.

My heart jolted as I read the name on the screen: Hi, it's Caroline. Stuart wants to help you. He's inviting you and your fiancée on our yacht this Wednesday. The Club is closed, but Stuart has access. He met Allison when he donated laptops to her school's needy kids. Stuart is sensitive to everyone's needs. He knows this is a challenging time and has the means to help. Please text me back either way. I want to make sure that you're okay.

CHAPTER TWENTY-SIX

A SUNRISE WITH ASH AND PIXIE DUST

JUNE 1, 2020

THE GYM

I sat on my bench and contemplated Caroline's proposal.

It was just after the break of dawn. The air was warm and moist, but the sea breeze was comforting. It was peaceful. I couldn't help thinking about accepting this invitation to meet The Monster. Sighing, I organized a reply as the waves caressed the shoreline.

Then, I felt a sharp pang with Ashley's morning text: **Allison was with that guy last night at the beach. I got us Starbucks. Be there shortly.**

Pressure built inside me while heating up at the words:

ALLISON

WAS

WITH

THAT

GUY

I felt the start of tears but was determined not to cry. Instead, I rubbed my face hard, wishing I had loved Allison less. It would've meant that I could've moved on. But I loved her deeply. Determined that this was a joke, I only stared at the text, waiting for a follow-up.

None came.

When I looked up from the screen again, ten minutes had passed, and Ashley was walking up. Her insistence that I cry it out didn't help as she sat beside me, handing me a Starbucks Dark Roast. My hands were too unsteady to take a sip. The thought of Allison with another man troubled me so much that I hadn't noticed Ashley was holding a joint.

"Since no one's around, I'm going to smoke this," she said. "So, my parents only started talking again to finalize the divorce." My chest tightened. To make matters worse, the soothing sea breeze died as she lit the joint. With a deep toke, she continued, "A good cry with caffeine goes a long way. Fuck it; you can even scream if you want. Just don't give up: Your love story is very different from theirs."

I scrutinized her for a second. "Are you sure it was Allison?"

Ashley looked at me. She hated to see the heartbreak that stalked me there in the present. "Yes, it was, but you're missing the big picture."

I ignored her. "Are you certain?"

She placed her Caffe Latte on the ground. "It was your fiancée walking with that same guy."

I couldn't stand what I was feeling. "Was she still wearing her ring?"

Ashley was on her feet in a flash. "STOP!" she yelled to snap me out of the funk. "Right now, it hurts. But in the end, Allison's experience with this guy will provide the clarity you both need."

"I never thought we'd be questioning so much."

Ashley picked up her Caffe Latte, swearing that there was a purpose for everyone we met. Her gut told her that Allison had to meet this guy to realize she couldn't replace me. "It's hell to anyone who risks it all for love," she insisted. "But it's the only way to begin again. You've done the right thing."

I glanced at my notepad next to me and thought. "There's nothing about this that feels right."

Ashley looked at me. With one hand pinching the joint, she raised the other with her Caffe Latte. She took a sip. Her eyes narrowed eerily, and her lips pursed. "Does your fiancée frequently smell your pillow?"

This girl eavesdrops on everything!

I played along, knowing she'd heard numerous conversations about Allison's attachment to my pillow. "How did you know that? I mean, yes. She does."

"That confirms my theory."

I grinned. "Go on...."

"When a woman is that drawn to a man's scent, it's a game changer. Your fiancée will soon reaffirm that you are her life's love."

"Interesting." I sighed heavily. "Must I reestablish that fact in all my books?"

"Only the ones that must completely shake up our lives to get us back to the love story we are meant to live. You know you've been less patient with her. You recently recalled a night at The Fish House when you discovered she had been communicating with Dr. Avery. That was in December. Before The Monster. Before the mayhem. You knew you had been living out a twisted version of your fairy tale that no woman could live up to." She paused and sighed. "Do you remember when I told you to love Allison exactly as she is?"

I nodded.

She continued, "When she feels appreciated again, you will live happily ever after…even in a pandemic." Her brown eyes widened at me. "I'm sorry. I should shut up."

Now I was sincerely taken aback. "No," I said, opening my notepad. "Please. Go on."

"Carla wrote that the test of true love is not when all is good. It's when all is flipped upside down in freaking pandemic mayhem. My parents didn't survive this," she said, shaking her head. "But they've never looked at each other like you guys do. Your love for each other has a fairy tale's magic and real-life heartache. And because of that, you and Allison keep fighting it out: An adult fairy tale, if you will. One in which you can hold onto your childhood dreams while living in this wild world. It's an inspiring story you can embrace because you've always believed." She paused, looked me in the eyes, and added, "Larry, this damn pandemic might be the best thing that happened to you two."

And then it all came together.

Our journey of love.

Even a magical love must be remade for each new chapter of our lives.

Repeatedly, Carla insisted that this was another love story. And she was right again.

"Hold on, Ashley," I said, rereading The Monster, Mayhem, & Magical Love line I recently wrote in my notepad. With a smile, I scribbled:

Book #3 Title: The Monster, Mayhem, & Magical Love.

"What did you write?" she asked, peering at my notepad.

Straightening, I said, "The title of book three. I see the story Carla intended for me to write."

Ashley's lips parted as she sucked in some salt air. "Good," she replied, gazing toward the orange and yellow sky. "Because your Tink will be back."

"I hope so."

She took a drag of her joint and shook her head. "No, you don't."

"I don't?" I asked, shifting my gaze to her, confused.

She pinched the joint and waved her hand. "You don't hope. You believe. YOU BELIEVE!"

I blinked at her, confused. "How high are you?"

"I'm not…look up!" Ashley grinned like a little girl. "Your pixie dust is starting to fall."

I stood up slowly, smelling smoke, and walked toward something coming down from the sky. "The wind's shifted. That's ash from the controlled burn across the river."

She took another toke and squinted into it. "We both know that's not all ash, Peter…."

CHAPTER TWENTY-SEVEN

I LOVE YOU!

JUNE 2, 2020

THE HOUSE

I stepped out of the shower to Ashley's morning text: **Allison was with that guy on Saturday night too. They had taught together for years.**

The house darkened.

I had to change the direction of my thoughts. Against my better judgment, I looked in the mirror over the bathroom sink. I couldn't take the sadness in my eyes. Struggling for a breath, I fell back against the bathtub. Tears rolled down my face. I refused to dry myself because I couldn't stop crying. Then another ping sounded. It sounded different. I peeked at the screen. It was Allison: **I miss you very much.**

I thought I heard the doorbell, so I wrapped a towel around my waist and hurried down the hall. As I approached the front door, it opened slowly. "Larry," Allison said, cocking her head just enough to make eye contact. Her eyes were blue, not bloodshot. She looked adorable, like my old Allison.

"Come in," I said. "Come in."

"Thanks."

"You look good," I added. "Great, in fact—" I paused, feeling a sudden wave of pain and nausea with thoughts of her new friend. "So, did you leave something behind?"

"Yes," she said gently. "I did leave something behind."

I fell silent. It took me a moment to steady myself as I swayed, lightheaded. It was too difficult to accept a future without Allison. "I'll help you find it," I said finally. "What is it?"

She gave me her sympathetic smile. "You." I didn't respond at all. I only watched her close the door. She turned back to me and continued, "This year has tested us. I was so focused on the hurt that all I was doing was suffering. I needed a break from that. From us. I've been hanging out with someone."

My pulse quickened. "I don't need those details."

"You do," she answered instantly. "Because he was someone who made me realize something." I heard the desperation in her voice and saw it in her eyes.

I sighed. "What is it?"

"You are the love of my life." I stood speechless as tears welled up in her eyes. She took a step toward me. "Do you still love me?"

"I do," I said, closing the distance between us. "I love you." We hugged each other tightly. Allison took a step back when we let go and pulled my towel off. Like a magnet, she was against me again. She looked up. I kissed her deeply. It was a beautiful yet haunting kiss that brought us together and highlighted how far apart we'd drifted. We both struggled to take off her clothes. Finally, we fell onto the couch and made love as if we hadn't done it in months. My mouth slowly slid down her body and up her thigh. She moaned joyfully as I tasted her and cried out as she came, shuddering hard. The sensation carried her away. Our bodies fit perfectly together, melding into one. And then my pent-up longing release was an exquisite pleasure that left me utterly spent. As our breathing settled, our gazes met. My senses were so scrambled that it took me a moment to clear my head. Then, I said, "Oh my God, I love you so much, Allison."

"I love you more," she replied, staring at me until our eyes eventually closed. We lay entwined, asleep in each other's arms.

Two hours later, she kissed me gently.

Kisses couldn't stop at just kisses when it came to Allison and me.

She pulled back, looked down, and said, "You are incredible. It's like you're sixteen." She grabbed hold of me. In a matter of minutes, I was inside of her again. We made passionate love. Twice. Then we spoke about her depression. My unrealistic expectations and lack of gratitude. Her girls. And my writing. With that, she grinned, grabbing her purse. She pulled out a copy of *The Gym*. "It was pre-ordered to my parents' house," she said, opening it to the chapter we first met. Then she read. "A spellbinding hush had fallen over the space. All I could hear was the whisper of my heart and the loveliest tinkle of bells." She kissed me again. "I am too sensitive. I mean, I'm sensitive. Please be more patient with me. I'm going to handle my issues. I promise. But you need to help me. Love me as you did back then." She stared at the pages of that chapter. "I miss this time desperately."

I nodded. "It was a special time."

She closed the book and smiled at me. "I love you more than I've loved anyone. We can't lose each other again." She pressed her face against my chest and then kissed me again. "Okay?"

My arms tightened around her, and I kissed her on her head. "Yes."

With a broad smile, I shifted my gaze to the coffee table as texts flashed on my screen. I assumed I had more member cancellations but was overjoyed when the book pre-orders landed. I hadn't smiled like this since the beginning of the year before everything changed after Carla's interview.

Minutes later, I received a Facebook notification: A member tagged me in a picture reading my book at the beach.

Then another.

Later that afternoon, we accepted Stuart's invitation. I had no plans to take anything from The Monster but didn't tell Allison that. I refused to share our dire finances either. I wanted to remain upbeat. Besides, I had to meet Stuart and figured an elegant evening on the river would help Allison and me; or, at the very least, entertain us.

We pulled into the Yacht Club at 6:00 and parked next to The Monster's 718 Boxster. We walked along the dock with heat lightning in the distance, marveling at the gorgeous vessels. When we passed Captain Hook's Jolly Roger, we noticed Caroline waving from, My Way, The Monster's new toy. She was leaning over the rail of the grandest yacht in the club, wearing a snappy summery outfit with Dior sunglasses.

"Welcome…welcome," she said, a bit buzzed while raising her champagne flute to us as we boarded. "We're glad you came."

I took a few steps and passed her on an adrenaline high. "Thanks for having us."

Allison added, "This is exquisite."

Caroline laughed. "You should see Stuart's Megayacht."

Allison glanced at me wide-eyed as we followed Caroline to the bar. She stared at a notecard she had been holding and looked poised to say something but smiled at us instead. "You guys are such a cute couple. I recall Larry living with his heart wide open, looking for the one. And now you found each other: Soulmates. The love of each other's lives. Any words of advice, Larry?"

I turned to Allison. "Well, magic happens when you don't give up, even when you want to."

My fiancée pulled me down for a kiss as Caroline placed the notecard on the bar and handed us a glass of champagne. "Let's raise our glasses to that instead: Cheers."

I wasn't sure what that was all about, but I could tell she was a romantic indeed. I nodded. "Cheers."

The crew members wore masks, but Caroline's was in her back pocket. She continued sipping the champagne while waiting for Stuart. When I finally asked where he was, I saw changes in her expression: The panic lurking at the edges of her mouth, the desperation in her eyes.

"He'll be here momentarily." Her voice was strained. "He always has to make a grand entrance."

I eyed her suspiciously. "I didn't think you drank alcohol."

"This year has taken its toll on me." She lowered her voice. "And so has Stuart."

One of the crew members whispered something in her ear. It was as if Big Brother was watching. A look at her convinced me that something was wrong. I sensed she didn't want us to accept anything from The Monster. I could tell she wanted to talk to me alone.

As I moved closer to her, Stuart flashed his perfected smile.

"Good evening, friends. Welcome to My Way!" His voice was strong and confident, like a politician's. He leaned in and kissed Allison on the cheek. No mask. No worries. His arrogance both infuriated and amused me. "Larry, your fiancée is gorgeous." Allison lit up like a Christmas tree as Stuart gripped my hand firmly. "I want to help you." He paused with a tight grip on my hand. "Okay, my friend?"

Why isn't this pompous prince practicing social distancing?

I smiled. "Has Dr. Folie sent word that the virus is dying with the summer heat?"

Stuart gestured to a CNN special report on the TV. "No, it is spreading rapidly," he said sternly. "However, we've all tested negative." He turned to Caroline. "Darling, did you not tell our guests to get tested before they boarded My Way?"

That seemed to surprise Caroline. Her perfectly arched eyebrows drew slightly together. "I thought I did." Her hand shook as she raised it for another sip. "My apologies."

Stuart did not practice social distancing or wear a mask outside his scripted media events. As Caroline looked annoyed, the charismatic man snapped fingers at the staff to top Allison's champagne off. He carried on about the day they met at her school. Allison's intellectual superiority shined as the two discussed Buddhism, ancient India, and mediation exercises. It was then Caroline had her chance to pull me aside. "Larry, would you like a tour around My Way?" she asked.

"You bet." I leaped up, anxious to hear her out. "Lead the way."

"Everything has gotten so out of hand," she whispered. "I'm not fond of Carla, but she's right. Stuart is a monster, and he played me like a fool. I've been speaking to my old boyfriend. The one you met at The Gym. I miss him." She paused uneasily. Her desire for him remained, which grew along with her guilt. "I screwed up badly. I'm scared. But Larry…." She took a breath and exhaled. "Do not take anything from Stuart. Don't give him an answer tonight."

I swallowed hard. "I didn't plan to." I glanced back at Allison. Stuart kept her champagne flute full. I sighed. "I know a lot. I also realize you don't want to hear Carla's name, but she nailed this guy perfectly. Her research on this virus cover-up has been spot-on. Scarily so."

Caroline paused, looking nauseous. "I know. But Carla didn't even get all the names linked to this mayhem. Please don't ask me either. I'll never speak about what I know…to anyone. It appalls me."

"Understood. But how are you planning on getting away from Stuart?" Caroline took her sunglasses off and blinked back tears. Every minute tightened something in her, and I thought she might break apart.

"Stuart thinks I have a sorority reunion in Napa."

Ashley, out of nowhere, hurried over.

"Hey, guys!" I was momentarily startled. I had forgotten that Stuart employed her. Ashley looked strange wearing his uniform and said, "Dinner is served."

I rolled my eyes. "Great," I said, shaking my head. "You look good in that uniform."

"Shut up." Ashley pushed me to the side. "I told you it was pixie dust. You and your Tinker Bell look great. You belong together." She nudged me further along. "Can I talk to you about something else?"

I nodded, and Caroline said, "I'll see you back at the table."

Ashley eyed Allison and said, "Since my mom suffers from depression and addiction, I see things you don't." She scooted closer. "Especially concerning your fiancée, and I get that you won't—"

"Ashley, hold on," I said, feeling a tightening in my chest. "Allison's been spending time with her parents and won't consume alcohol in front of her father—"

"What does that mean?"

"It means my fiancée is not like your mother."

"Larry, my mom went months without incident, and then something would trigger her depression, and insanity would consume our home. The next day, my dad would find empties in her closet and destructive emails on her laptop. My mom would swear my dad was the problem, but she lied about everything to keep her addiction going. I turned to books as an outlet when I was eleven. I wasn't going to say anything, but the entire staff has commented that Stuart is keeping Allison's flute full of his vintage Dom Perignon."

I sighed. "Thanks for your concern, but the drinking is under control."

She gestured to Allison, tipping back her flute, tipsy. "Okay."

I straightened, glaring at her. "Are we done?"

Ashley rolled her eyes. "Fine, Peter, keep flying back to Never Land to avoid all the uglies of this wild world—just don't cry when I tell you I told you so." She hit my arm. "Walk with me. There's something else."

I drew in a steadying breath.

She continued, "Tyler's been texting me. Sharky's not doing well. His liver is failing—" The Monster cut her off,

"Ashley," he shouted. "Stop harassing our guests. And open another bottle of Dom."

"Yes, sir!" she snapped. Then she whispered to me, "I hate him."

Two hours later, after Stuart's sales pitch to save us, I told him we weren't making rash decisions. He stood increasingly irritated and swirled the Insignia in his Riedel glass. "Your fitness center cannot remain open without my help. I would strongly consider my offer." The anger he was trying to stifle made me nervous. Finally, The Monster stepped forward and announced that he had to make a call. He marched off like a schoolyard bully who didn't get his way, taking his ball and going home.

Meanwhile, Caroline drank Grey Goose from a soda cup to further infuriate him. I circled back to Allison after Stuart groaned when Caroline tilted her head and blew cigarette smoke into the air. I needed to prevent what felt like an inevitable calamity.

I eyed the clock and leaned into Allison. "We should get going."

She shook her head. "It's early."

With Ashley's warning on my mind, I tried again. "Allison, please. We've had enough to drink."

"You told me you wouldn't act like my father tonight."

A surge of protectiveness permeated me, head to toe. I reached for Allison's hand and took a calming breath. "I love you. We should go."

My heart leaped a little in my chest when she didn't pull away, but instead, she tugged me closer to her side. Although the alcohol caused her to struggle with dark thoughts, she said, "I love you. Let's go."

CHAPTER TWENTY-EIGHT

AN INEVITABLE END

SUMMER 2020

The following morning, I woke at dawn.

I rolled over to face Allison. The sight of my love beside me was all I needed. Regardless of being a romantic, I didn't quite get how much her imperfections were marks of authenticity. And that was her true beauty. There was nothing more rare or beautiful than a woman being unapologetically herself. I couldn't help but smile as I stared at her, finally accepting her perfect imperfection. As Allison's eyes fluttered open, I whispered, "I love you."

"I love you more."

"I want you to know I'm in for the good, the bad, and the ugly, Allison."

"Good, because I really don't want to hurt any more guys trying to replace you," she replied, biting down on a smile. After pulling up a song on her phone, she started singing Shania Twain's "You're Still the One." Halfway through the song, our gazes shifted to three simultaneous texts.

Since it was Tyler, I read them aloud, stunned: Sharky's dead.
His liver failed him.

Anyway, he liked you, and I thought you should know.

Storm clouds thickened as I responded with my deepest condolences. In many ways, I felt Sharky was finally in a better place because he'd been living in so much pain. Allison could tell I was emotional and snuggled close. I looked into her blue eyes and couldn't catch my breath for a heartbeat. She kissed my cheek and then kissed my lips and neck. Within minutes we took off our clothes and started to make love. Ten minutes later, with rain coming down sideways, we rolled off each other, breathing heavily.

Then another text flashed on my screen: It was Tyler thanking me. I wrapped a towel around my waist and typed: How are you and Carla?

Right after I hit the arrow, I saw the dots indicating that he was responding.

I began pacing, and it appeared. We're glad to see you're back with Allison. Even your magical love must be remade for each new chapter of your life. Keep that in mind as you shift your focus to defeat The Monster. We can't wait to see how your fairy tale ends. Good luck!

I sighed and then laughed as it dawned on me that Tyler was getting weekly updates from Ashley.

Throughout the rest of June, The Monster had the landlord pressure me for the rent owed. Although the only money coming in was from my book sales, it was enough to stall the inevitable. It was also something that further infuriated Stuart. Caroline insisted that his temper had worsened since the night we met on the yacht. His fits of rage were the scariest days of her life. Luckily, she got away from him unscathed. Caroline considered that a personal triumph while refusing to talk about the cover-up.

At the end of June, I received a text from her. It included a picture of her old boyfriend fishing in the Keys: Hi Larry! I'm enjoying a new love with an old friend. Yes, the guy who fell off your treadmill and almost ended up in the nail salon. We're going to be weird, goofy, old people. And I love it! XOXO Caroline.

I stiffened, unsure if I was truly happy for her.

How could I allow myself to wonder that?

The bitter thoughts I had surrounding her scripted visit to The Gym had everything to do with The Monster's manipulation of her. Looking back, Caroline had to be one of his easiest targets. I remembered her sitting across from me during *The Gym's* storyline, searching for her perfect love, clueless that she'd already found him. The journey of love is the greatest adventure of all. And I was happy she got this second chance.

I smiled and replied: True love doesn't go away. They might go unseen and heard for a while but always return. I am happy for you, Caroline!

My heart constricted with her follow-up: Thank you, Larry. We're drinking a bottle of Josh and enjoying your love story. Cheers!

That was the last time I heard from Caroline Haines.

By July, the fitness center was so hot that I was finishing a bottle of Evian every hour to stay hydrated. When I went home in the evenings, Allison would stare at me with an exhausted look. My worry was evident even in the pale glow of the light on the lanai.

"Larry, there's no end to this," Allison repeated nightly, reaching for my hand to console me. "What are we going to do?"

A month after the Black Lives Matter protests broke out across the country, data from the largest U.S. cities found no evidence that the virus had spiked. Despite that information, Dr. Folie warned a Senate committee that the number of new cases in the U.S. could rise from forty thousand to one hundred thousand by Labor Day. While certain members were laughing at this guy, many others were hanging on his every word.

At the end of July, I was ecstatic that many members enjoyed my book, but I was devastated that they couldn't return to The Gym. I became increasingly torn after listening to each voicemail:

Beep.

Larry, it's Barb Miller. Your book brought back such beautiful memories. Unfortunately, I will not make any new ones until the vaccines are out. Dr. Folie is advising that we stay home and stay safe.

Beep.

Hi Larry, it's Kate Dowling. I loved the book! That was a special time at The Gym. I want to return, but I can't right now. I hope to see you after the vaccines are available. I hope you can hold on. Stay safe, Larry.

Beep.

I laughed, and I cried. Wonderful book! I am so happy you found your Tinker Bell. This is Jo Ann Smith. Wishing you guys well. I hope to see you after we can be vaccinated, Larry. Stay safe, dear.

Beep.

We made it to August.

Many states, including New York, California, and Michigan, postponed reopening plans. There was no way around what was happening. During the dog days of summer, the space rapidly aged from the rust. The doors were open to the salt air for too long. Several pairs of unfamiliar eyes stared back at me, cleaning the equipment and wondering how long I could hold out. Most people working out at The Gym were all escapees from New York, New Jersey, Michigan, and even two middle-aged couples from California and Oregon. They all insisted there was more to this virus and its mandates than anyone could explain. Listening to them vent, I could only shrug at the whirlwind of chaos.

"If you want science, follow the money!" one would yell when he'd stretch out under Dr. Folie's updates. "Can you say vaccines?"

On the first day of September, my alarm went off at 5:30 as it did every morning. With a groan, I woke up, not realizing that they were getting louder and angrier each day. I lived this routine for more days than I wanted to count. There were no set hours when we were open. It all depended on when I got there and how long I could endure the heat. This Tuesday, I strode in at 8:00, and a heavy-set man in his mid-sixties immediately followed.

He stared at me for an awkward moment. "You must be Larry."

I nodded, feeling faint. "How can I help you?"

"You already did. I'm here because of your book, *The Gym*," he said, dropping a weight belt on the check-in counter. "At first, I wasn't sure if this place was real. But I knew I had to spend some time here when I found out it was."

My eyes widened at his statement as my phone pinged with Allison's text: **Stuart invited me to brunch on the yacht. My phone's about to die. I'm sure I'll have some juicy material for book #3! LOL! Talk to you soon. I love you!**

I blinked back at the man. "Well," I said distractedly. "Welcome to The Gym."

He introduced himself as Michael—a restaurateur whose business never reopened. As an entrepreneur, I could tell he was taken aback by the equipment's poor condition and wanted to help. He understood that the story he had recently read was from a different time, a special time. Michael pulled his wallet from a knapsack.

"Here," he said, handing me a hundred-dollar bill. "I'll have another one for you tomorrow. I'm thrilled to be here."

"Thank you," I said, taking the money gratefully. "Where are you from?"

"Michigan." He frowned. "It's a place where most people wouldn't know tyranny if it covered their faces, locked them in their homes, and enacted the biggest wealth transfer in history." He paused and shook his head. "And I say that as a registered Democrat." I stood speechless while texting Allison to call me. Michael squinted over my shoulder at pictures of her on the wall and continued, "When two souls are meant to connect, timing and circumstances are all irrelevant." He nodded. "It is magical. I enjoyed your story. But I didn't think your girl would actually look like Tinker Bell. That's uncanny."

I grinned. "Magical."

He stared at me for a long moment. "Indeed. Have you given much thought to preserving the wonderful memories of this place in your book while moving on?"

"It's...difficult," I choked out. "Have you read my first book?"

"I just ordered it," he replied, running a hand across the stubble on his jaw. "Why?"

"Well, there was a girl...named Wendy."

He swiveled his head around to ensure no one was behind him and said, "You had a Wendy and a Tinker Bell in back-to-back books?" I nodded. He continued, "Let me guess...that one didn't end as well." I shook my head. He tightened his weight belt and headed over to the free weights. "Well, at least you now have a pandemic...that should provide some interesting material for a continuation."

If you only knew.

I sighed, stuffed the c-note in my pocket, and blinked at Ashley's back-to-back texts: **Have you seen the sexual harassment charges against Stuart?**

He read the excerpt I sent the staff and knows he'll be exposed as The Monster in your new book. My friend said your words caused him to cut a chair with his collectible Saber in half while swearing that he'd get revenge.

My heart was going a mile a minute as I hurried over to the TVs. The local news station interviewed a woman from Hook's firm who filed the latest sexual harassment charge against The Monster.

When I raised the volume, Aurora's voice startled me from behind. "Boss, did you see all the women coming forward with harassment charges against Stuart Grossman—" She peered intently at the woman being interviewed, which rendered her speechless.

I took a sip of water and felt increasingly woozy.

Then another text caused me to twitch. Again, it was Ashley: **Allison's on the yacht with The Monster! They're pulling out now.**

With a rush of adrenaline, I sent Allison another text: **Get off that boat! The Monster has come undone.**

Aurora watched The Gym as I ran out of it.

Then Ashley called. I answered, "Where are you?"

"I'm heading back to the yacht club with Jimmy." I paused for a second, thinking.

"Jimmy, who?"

"Your old nemesis, Captain Hook. Meet us at the Jolly Roger. He wants to help."

CHAPTER TWENTY-NINE

A ROUGH DAY AT SEA!

SEPTEMBER 1, 2020

THE YACHT CLUB

"Stuart knows the end is near," Ashley insisted. "He'll turn himself in and hide behind his legal team." I tried to take strength from that, to believe it honestly, but any hope was becoming difficult to hold on to. The Monster's yacht was gone, and my fiancée was on it. Each passing minute had weakened me.

I blinked away the dots you get before you pass out.

Stay strong.

STAY STRONG!

I took a few breaths, told myself I was all right, didn't believe it, and went on to the Jolly Roger. Hook fell into step beside me. For a moment, I tensed up. Then he placed a reassuring hand on my shoulder.

"I still have a soft spot for your fiancée and want to help."

"You partnered with a monster."

"That's over," he said reassuringly. "I will make certain that nothing happens to Allison."

My fear was overshadowed by sheer bewilderment. "I-I tried warning her," I sputtered. "She never charges her phone."

Hook paused. "Why?"

"Allison misplaces everything," Ashley said, coming up behind us. "Larry calls her cell to find it, but there's never enough time to charge it before she leaves for school."

Hook's gaze slowly shifted to Ashley and then back to me.

I felt my mouth fall open. Then I couldn't help but smile, thinking about Allison's chaotic morning ritual. I turned to Ashley; my thoughts were in such disarray. "Ashley, can you call The Monster's crew?"

"I have been," she replied, checking her texts. "No one is answering."

"All aboard!" Hook shouted, putting his long black hair up in a ponytail. "They are heading for the inlet. We need to hurry; a bad storm is brewing."

Just then, we were on our way. As the Jolly Roger cruised down the river, I realized we had to do this mission alone because The Monster had the police chief in his back pocket. I shook off that thought as Ashley pointed to something on the cabin's wall. Upon a closer look, I noticed Mr. Smee's striped T-shirt in a protective case, with an engraving that read: Rest in Peace – Connor Lee –1974 – 2017.

I swallowed hard and eyed Captain Hook. "So…Captain…." I cleared my throat. "Hook…James, are we attempting some sort of citizen arrest?"

Hook shook his head sympathetically. "No, today an old friend will be helping us," he said. "Don't worry. We'll get your Tinker Bell back."

Visibly amused, Ashley tilted her head at him. "You said Tinker Bell."

"Ashely," Hook exhaled gruffly, "Go to the bow and rest your mouth."

"Aye, aye, Captain!" she added. "The Monster's going to freak when he sees you two together. Captain Hook and Peter Pan Man! Oh, geez...."

We were out at sea. The number of houses slowly thinned until there was no sign of civilization. The late summer sky darkened, and the temperature dropped drastically. I squinted into the ocean spray as the winds picked up. I could barely see the tall coconut palms that dotted the deserted shoreline. It felt like we had a better chance of finding a needle in a haystack than The Monster's My Way with my girl.

"Mr. Smee," Captain Hook bellowed. "Give me a sign!"

Oh God, now I'm hearing things.

Hook repeated himself. "Mr. Smee, give me a sign!"

Why is he calling to a dead man?

Cold fear shot through my gut.

What is happening?

Captain Hook tried to steady the Jolly Roger, but the winds roared in off the open water, and the rain pelted down.

I wiped my face and gripped the side. "Where is Ashley?"

"MR. SMEE," Hook repeated himself, yet again, only louder. "GIVE ME A SIGN!"

Lightning lit up the darkened sky.

The Monster's yacht was dead ahead. I yelled, "There they are!" With the rain coming down sideways, I wiped my face with my hand, thinking I had lost it. For a second, it appeared that Ashely was a mermaid swimming toward The Monster's yacht. I shook free of that image and turned to My Way as Hook maneuvered the Jolly Roger beside it. I took a calming breath and leaped aboard.

As lightning flickered and thunder boomed, I heard the loveliest tinkle of bells.

I slipped on broken glass, moving toward my Tinker Bell. The vessel appeared to have been ransacked by pirates. Or something. Then I twisted to her whimper.

Allison.

She stood up. Tears gathered in her eyes. "Larry, he has a sword!" Allison shrieked.

At her words, I blinked. "Where is he?"

"Behind you!"

I spun to The Monster glaring at me. His skin was as white as paper. His forehead was cut; dried blood framed his dark-ringed eyes.

"You are a naïve fool, Pan Man. Look around," he growled, staring at me. "The world has gone dark. How do you intend to expose all the powerful people involved in this cover-up?"

I yelled, "One monster at a time!" My voice sounded like the real Peter Pan, so I cleared my throat and tried again. "ONE MONSTER AT A TIME!"

Much better.

He slid the sword across his hand, and blood gushed to the floor as rage coiled in his eyes like a snake ready to strike. "You could've taken my money and saved your gym," he roared. "But you chose to keep writing. Your belief in love prevailing when everything else fails will be your demise. This pandemic is about power and control, not passion and pixie dust. People want to have decisions made for them. I am part of a group of elites who will ensure that happens. Stop fighting it, Pan Man!"

My breathing was quick and shallow, and thoughts fell on one another as I studied this tortured soul. Finally, I said, "Stuart, put the sword down. You don't want to hurt anyone else."

"Why? Carla and Caroline are gone. Everyone's betrayed me."

"Life might be trying to teach you something…a lesson that's never too late to learn."

"Oh, no. It's too late. People were crueler than I ever imagined when I was a boy."

"But they could be kinder and more loving than you've ever dreamed. We can get you help."

A ray of light appeared through the swirling clouds.

"This virus was necessary. It killed off the weak. Only the strong should survive. I am not a monster: I am a savior." He took a step toward me. "You are a pathetic romantic who has filled this dark world with false hope. No magical love will save you now." He raised his sword. "Prepare to die, Pan Man!" I dropped to the floor as The Monster swung his sword and missed. Panic clawed at me as Allison raised her hand, cringing in terror. I took hold of it. "Oh, how sweet," The Monster seethed. "Now, you and your Tink will die a gruesome death together."

A sharp gust of wind knocked him backward and into Captain Hook as he emerged from the Jolly Roger. Hook tossed him to the side like a sack of potatoes, looked up to the heavens, and bellowed, "MR. SMEE, DESTROY THIS MONSTER!"

The floor buckled and heaved as a lightning bolt struck down. The flash momentarily blinded me. I heard Allison's voice, but I wasn't sure where she was. Slowly, I stood up as pixie light flew around me.

My gaze shifted to the clearing sky as my second star to the right shone so bright.

I felt like I was in *The Wizard of Oz* when the movie went from black and white to color. A magnificent rainbow appeared over Hook as he said, "Rest assured, The Monster is dead."

Then, "Sweetie—" I jolted awake.

"Tink—I mean, Allison...."

My fiancée continued, "You were dreaming."

I rubbed my face. "Did Stuart invite you on his yacht?"

"Yes, but I wasn't going to go. Aurora called me to The Gym after you passed out. Do you remember?"

"No."

Calmly, Allison explained that she had brought me home in a terrible storm. I had been asleep for hours. And then she mentioned Hook.

While processing the dream, I confirmed. "Captain Hook?"

She smiled. "Yes. Hook wants to help you. He offered you a position to run his new liquor store."

I hesitated. "Really?"

She nodded. "And Stuart was struck by lightning on his yacht."

I touched her face to make sure this wasn't another dream. "Say that again."

She pulled my hand off her face and kissed it. "Larry, The Monster is dead."

I sat up slowly. "Mr. Smee...."

"What?"

"It's uh—just a dream that came true."

•　　•　　•

Three weeks later, I blinked back tears as Aurora took one last picture of me in The Gym. Emotions overwhelmed me — love for my beloved fitness center most of all. The memories that rushed over me were impossible to ignore. I gripped the keys and released my breath; she knew then that I was holding it, waiting. With one hand leaning on the door to steady myself, I locked it with the other.

I choked back a tiny sob. "I intended on retiring here."

Aurora smiled back at me the best she could, knowing it would be our last time at The Gym. "Sometimes the places we wanted in all of our stories are only meant to be in a couple of books," she said. "And that's okay."

Don't cry.

I couldn't hold back my tears. "I'm going to miss you." I nodded as they streamed down my face. "I really can't imagine not seeing you in this place."

She blinked back her watery eyes and hurried over to hug me. "I promised myself I wouldn't cry."

I squeezed her tight. "It's probably best we just say goodbye."

"Goodbye, boss."

"Goodbye, Aurora."

CHAPTER THIRTY

THE WEDDING

NOVEMBER 2021

ST. AUGUSTINE

It was a year later.

The coastal clouds turned silver, reflecting the moon as they rolled across the evening sky. As they thickened, I turned the page of my worn notepad. It was appropriate that I reflected on our love prevailing in this dark fairy tale from the porch of the bed and breakfast hosting our elopement weekend. Allison spent months searching for the perfect wedding location. When my favorite educator decided on St. Augustine, the oldest city in the United States, I immediately agreed. We seemed to be planning this event shortly after meeting on a stormy Sunday, the first day of October 2017. It wasn't just a first date, however. It was the day we became inseparable.

Since then, we've made a million memories, each day with a different soundtrack, cherishing every song. Looking back over these four years, it was evident that we refused to give up on each other.

Although this often-intense journey has stretched and tangled the bond between us, it has never broken, which proved that what we found in one another couldn't be replaced. We missed The Gym but were grateful for the opportunity that Hook granted me to run his liquor store. I had time to write while considering the impact of this never-ending pandemic. Perhaps it's true that the darkest moments of those days changed this storyline. As the early chapters indicated, our problems amplified when I completed *The Gym's* manuscript while releveling in the fitness center's newfound success. Ironically, Allison pondered life without a lockdown; she suggested that we might not have taken the necessary steps to fix all that had gone awry with us while joking that I might've ended up with Ashley.

These days, Ashley was editing manuscripts and tirelessly working on book three. I grinned at Ashley's latest text: **I hope you're enjoying your wedding weekend, but I need another chapter of The Monster, Mayhem, & Magical Love, please!**

Inside, I could tell Allison had returned from her shopping spree when her 90s playlist blared out of her laptop speakers. Soon after, she danced to "Groove Is in the Heart" on the porch while wearing a groovy new blouse.

"Do you like it?"

I smiled. "It's beautiful."

"This might sound crazy, but I think I saw Carla holding an infant when I was paying."

I blinked, thinking I must've misunderstood her. "What did you say?"

"I saw Carla Kimbrel holding a baby."

I mulled it over. "Maybe she's been hiding in St. Augustine this entire time."

Allison released a heavy sigh. "Oh God, what're the chances she haunts our beautiful wedding?"

I pushed myself up and kissed my bride-to-be.

"No, it's doubtful that it was her," I said, checking the time. "Our dinner reservation is in twenty minutes." I glanced down the street to ensure that Carla wasn't watching us from under a streetlight. "We should get going." I wiped my suddenly sweaty forehead and rushed us out the door.

After dinner, we strolled along the bayfront, laughing, reminiscing, and taking cute selfies by the water. It turned out to be a fabulous autumn evening. Allison ran up to the Gazebo, where we would read our vows, ecstatic at how tastefully decorated it was. I wandered around it while acknowledging the grounds were exquisitely manicured for our pictures.

Allison came down the steps; she was glowing. "This is perfect."

I smiled at her. "It is."

The next morning, I opened the curtains, and the sunlight came streaming into our room.

The day has finally arrived!

I smiled as I put on a robe to pick up the breakfast tray at our door, stuffed French toast drizzled in syrup with a side of fruit. It looked too pretty to eat. I put a plate beside Allison, still sleeping at 10:00, and kissed her cheek. "It's our wedding day," I whispered. "Hip, hip, hooray." I poured some coffee and went onto the porch. We decided on an elopement package with an early afternoon ceremony. I checked on my suit with butterflies to ensure it was still hanging just right.

Then I heard Allison cursing under her breath. Seconds later, she shouted, "Larry, call my phone."

I spilled my coffee. "Sure." As it rang in my ear, I sighed. "Anything?"

"No."

I drew in a slow breath. "You had it at the restaurant last night."

"Have you seen it since?"

"No." My eyes closed when I got her voicemail. "You must have left it there."

"I know!" Her voice was frantic. "My makeup lady is coming in thirty minutes."

"Don't worry," I said reassuringly. "I'll get it."

At 10:30, I jogged up the bayfront wall. The city noise was the sound of horse hoofs and trolley bells. St. Augustine didn't have potted plants, but a city built around plants, and St. George Street was where the downtown's hustle, bustle, and beauty converged. I pushed through the crowd, crossing over Cathedral Place, hoping to beat them to St. George Street. I sidestepped an older woman walking her dog and ran into a younger one pushing a stroller.

"I'm sorry," I muttered, glancing back at the stroller.

Still upright, keep moving.

"Larry?"

I stopped.

I turned slowly because I knew the voice. It had haunted me since her last call nearly two years before. She removed her Florida Gator cap, and I squinted so it wouldn't be so obvious.

"Carla?"

She took a step toward me. "Hey, how are you?"

I met her eyes and felt warm in a way I hadn't expected. "I'm good…I'm getting married."

"I know." She shrugged. "I still stalk Allison's Facebook page. I recognized her shopping yesterday. It's crazy that you chose to marry in St. Augustine."

I nodded. "Well…this has been a crazy storyline," I said, walking around to the front of the stroller.

"You can't say I didn't warn you."

I could only nod and smile as I peeked into the stroller. "Is this your baby?"

She pulled her bundle of joy out and held her tight. "Yes, this is Addison."

"She's adorable."

Carla beamed. "Say hi to Peter Pan Man, Addison!"

I winced as heads turned and put my finger in Addison's hand. She started kicking and smiling. "Hi, Addison." My gaze shifted to Carla, wondering who the father was. "So, who chose the name?"

Carla's lips edged into a smile. "Tyler."

I grinned. "I haven't heard from him in a while. Is he okay?"

"Yes." She drew in a breath. "He wanted me to explain everything to you, but I, uh…I couldn't."

There was an awkward pause.

"It's okay. This adventure has taught me some valuable lessons."

She nodded, thinking. "It's so weird that I knew you would get it," she said, seemingly going back over it in her mind. "When Stuart found out that Shawn was talking to your fiancée, he set us up on a date. The Monster manipulated everything. The doctor helped me research the story, but I was never into him. I was more upset that he was close to Allison. Deep down, I never doubted your love for her. I was just miserable. All the while knowing you were the only one who could write this story as a fairy tale." She paused and stared at me. Her eyes pleaded for forgiveness. "But then all that bad stuff happened."

I raised my eyebrows. "In the future, you should be open to bad stuff leading to better things…you'll be surprised how things turn out."

Her mouth twitched like she'd forced back a smile. "Stuart hated you because your youthful spirit irritated his demons. He knew you'd expose him as a monster."

I visualized Carla's Instagram post that began book three and said, "Fairy tales were never meant to be sweet stories with little substance. From an early age, fairy tales intended to teach us that monsters exist. They show us that these evil creatures can be defeated. That is the power of a story."

Relief flashed in her eyes. "That is the power of a fairy tale!" We smiled at each other. Still holding her baby, she gave me a one-arm hug. "I cried when Ashley told me the title of book three was *The Monster, Mayhem & Magical Love*."

I threw a thumb over my shoulder. "That love won't be so magical if I don't get back to my Tink."

Carla nodded, blinking back watery eyes. "Last night, I dreamt I would see you today."

I took a few steps backward. "Dreams do come true," I said. "If we wish hard enough."

She laughed and wiped her eyes. "Goodbye, Peter…sorry, Larry."

I smiled as Carla lifted Addison's hand to wave goodbye to me.

"Goodbye, girls."

Thirty minutes later, I raced up the path to our bed and breakfast. The staff was tending to the light, airy sheer backdrop around the Gazebo, and for the first time, I could envision Allison and me exchanging rings and vows.

Our room's sizable wooden door creaked as I pushed it open.

"Honey, I'm home."

Allison was getting her makeup done and yelled at me in the mirror, "Don't look at my dress!"

"Don't worry; I can't take my eyes off you."

"Aww…seriously?"

I nodded. "You look radiant," I said, hurrying by her to shower. "I'll change in the bathroom."

"In a few hours, we'll be married," she gushed.

I smiled. "I'm so happy."

"Me too."

Soon after, I walked outside to the photographer taking pictures of the stunning flowers and candles inside the Gazebo. On this day, the whole garden seemed to glow. As the music began, the whispers to take my place had me rushing up the steps. I turned around and noticed tourists stopping in awe of someone approaching.

Then my heart skipped a beat.

It was Allison.

My bride had a light glowing from within: Breathtaking was the first word that came to mind. She walked up against the beautiful bayfront in the most elegant wedding gown I could have imagined. Exquisite lace accented her blonde hair and blue eyes, and her long lace sleeves disappeared into the autumn bouquet she carried. I grinned from ear to ear, frozen in a dreamlike state. Everyone around

Allison reflected her smile as she approached the Gazebo, nodding that they were in the midst of an enchanting bride. I reached my hand to help her up the steps and into a moment where time stood still. Our vows, kisses, and chemistry were so heartfelt that even the staff shed a tear.

And then, in a flurry of pixie dust, we walked off as husband and wife.

A magical love....

EPILOGUE

AUGUST 2022

It was seventy-nine days until our anniversary.

I finished my coffee at the kitchen table, haunted by the warnings I refused to heed. It felt like we were back in the middle of the pandemic. My gaze shifted from Allison's remorseful morning texts to too many empty wine bottles on the counter to Dr. Folie preaching about vaccines and mask mandates.

As Carla predicted, a growing number of critics proved he was an unhinged, unelected bureaucrat who deserved to be fired for his lies, malfeasance, and inability to address the virus properly. Although his hostility towards transparency had many Americans tuning out his tyrannical tirades, it didn't stop him from lashing out at legislators who dared question his role in this never-ending pandemic.

I turned off the TV and scribbled on the last page of my worn notepad: *One monster at a time.*

With thunder rumbling in the distance, I shifted in the chair to our framed wedding picture. I stared at it, recalling that blissful weekend while anxiously tapping the pen on that page. I envisioned an epilogue that captured our marital felicity a year after our wedding, but I found myself having to let go of what I thought should happen.

Breathe.

This storyline tested me in ways I could've never imagined.

Stay strong.

My hand shook as I wrote the notes for a new epilogue:

All that glitters is not gold ~William Shakespeare

That tiny flicker of light in Allison's tunnel of darkness hadn't been seen in days. One moment, she was happy and serene. The next moment, she was brimming with rage. I felt like I was in this insidious race with something that had taken over my wife's life. I kept reminding myself that she was a great partner with whom I shared this magical love...if only. If only she didn't have this problem–

My head jerked up, startled by my wife entering the kitchen. I placed the pen down, with a queasy feeling in my stomach. I could barely see any blue in her bloodshot eyes. I rose to Allison, seized by the fear that my best friend was about to hit rock bottom. In the insanity of the last few days, she had lost her teaching certification, and as her alcohol-related issues mounted, her anxiety and depression worsened. I would come home from work wanting to scream at her and hug her at the same time.

On this dreary Sunday, I stared down at her and saw the wrenching emotion in her eyes, the regret of her actions sober. Her lower lip trembled. "I'm sorry about last night," she said under her breath. "I was on the verge of a nervous breakdown."

Looking at her hurt so much I could hardly breathe. With my composure crumbling, I focused on damage control. "You should check what you did on the internet," I said, trying not to sound sullen. "There are posts you'll want to delete."

Tears filled her eyes. "I-I know." Her voice was shaky. "I had a moment."

My heart ached. "I thought we were done with those moments."

She sniffled, wiping her eyes. "Well, I thought you were done with your book."

I opened my mouth to respond, but tears squeezed past my eyelashes.

Allison sniffled louder. "I know you're rewriting the epilogue," she continued. "I realize it's because you no longer believe we'll live happily ever after. You're the only man who came close to convincing me I had a chance of living one out…so pat yourself on the back…" her voice trailed off, staring at me.

I saw my own emotions mirrored in her eyes: fear, sadness, pity. I touched my soulmate's face gently. "We can still live out our happily ever after. But life is tough. It often sucks. That's a reality I'm grateful you reminded me of, so please understand we can fix this problem."

Lighting lit up the darkened room.

"You told me you love my imperfections."

I pulled her tight against me. "I do, but this is different."

"It's just my Bohemian ways."

"Allison, we need to get a handle on the alcohol."

At the mention of that, she sobbed uncontrollably. "It's this never-ending pandemic," she mumbled, holding me tightly. "You agreed."

"I don't want to hear about the pandemic. Drinking with you through that mayhem was the worst thing I could've done."

She looked up at me. "Larry, for two years, people have been drinking excessively."

I drew in a breath, hoping I didn't look as irritated as I felt. "Allison, you're a beautiful, talented woman who will shine once we address this problem."

She took a step backward, shaking her head. "I need you to stop overreacting."

I looked out the window as a steady rain ran down it, like tears. I wanted to say more, but I only reminded her to delete her problematic posts. She couldn't help herself; she let out a whimper of sound. I swallowed hard. "I put your laptop on the coffee table when I cleaned up your broken wine glass."

Allison stiffened. Her pain was reflected in her gaze. Then, she turned to her laptop, brushed the moist trail from her skin, and hurried to erase any evidence confirming she had come undone.

Before I could say anything else, a text pinged my phone on the kitchen table. Snatching it up, I noticed an unknown number. For some reason, I felt compelled to read the message: Larry, it's Carla. This is my new number.

I flinched as her follow-up flashed in my hand.

Ashley spent the weekend with me. She told me about your wife's struggles. Like Sharky and Ashley's mother, my sister fought mental illness and addiction and lost everything. It's more common than you'd think. My sister became so close to her addiction that leaving it behind would have been like killing the part of herself that taught her how to survive. I pray Allison is not at that point. Call me if you would like to talk. I would hate to see you lose that magical love.

A chill spread through me.

Finally, Allison closed her laptop and shifted uncomfortably on the couch. "Who texted you?"

Tears stung my eyes. "Ashley," I lied, hoping to calm my fragile wife. "It was just Ashley."

"Is she okay?" Allison asked, her demeanor changing as she approached me.

I wiped my eyes. "Yes."

"So, why are you crying?"

I stared at her in disbelief. "You refuse to hear what I'm saying," I said, my voice rising. "We cannot continue living this way." I took a breath and exhaled. "This can ruin our marriage."

Allison looked like a lost little girl, worried I'd endured too much. She glanced at my notepad, thinking. Then she said, "Our magical love can withstand anything…you wrote it." Her voice rose. "Right, Larry?"

I ached to say yes, to scream it, but I couldn't even nod.

My wife's frown lifted, and a cold, stark fear widened in her eyes. "You want to crucify me," she added harshly. "I refuse to allow you to tell me how I can live. It's controlling. It's abuse."

"Controlling," I gasped. "Abuse?"

"Yes!" she cried. "Now, I'll never believe there can be a happily ever after in this wild world."

God help us.

I looked into my wife's scared eyes, knowing Carla had a point. I also realized Allison didn't break easily. Seeing myself in her eyes, I felt we could do this.

Together.

Faith.

As my gaze shifted across the room, I sought to reassure her with her words and our wedding picture. I walked over to it, grabbed it, and returned to her. "You are right."

"About what?"

"Our magical love. It will give us the strength we need to get through this."

Her mouth wavered. "You don't understand my pain." She squeezed her watery eyes shut. "You don't…."

"I don't," I admitted. "But I've done some research on this—"

Her eyes burst open. "It's too late." She sniffled hard. "So, STOP!"

Silence settled between us.

Breathe.

My voice fell to a whisper. "Allison, I can't stop."

"Why?" she sobbed. "I ruined our love story."

"No, you didn't." I placed our wedding picture on the table. "All the best love stories have one thing in common."

She took a deep, steadying breath. "What is it?"

"You have to go against the odds to get there."

The rain stopped.

She looked at me through the eyes I remembered.

I drew back, admiring them.

The sky brightened.

"I-I can't imagine living without you, Larry," she murmured. "Do you remember telling me it would be a privilege to grow old with me?"

I nodded. "I meant it."

She sniffled. "Aside from the months around our wedding, these pandemic years have been the most difficult of my life."

"Can we focus on the future and get healthy together?"

"I promise I'll try."

Hope.

I wiped the tears streaming down my face, only focused on this tiny step forward, praying it would lead to the biggest step of our lives, and said, "I love you."

Allison's glassy eyes opened to her soul. "I love you more."

THE END

ABOUT THE AUTHOR

After many early successes as a salesman, Lawrence H. Sola moved on to the wine industry in 1994. In 2009, his career inspired him to write his first novel, *The Show (Peter Pan Man Book 1)*. Shortly after *The Show* was released, he purchased a fitness center that became the backdrop to his sequel, *The Gym (Peter Pan Man Book 2)*, along with the third installment of his book series: *The Monster, Mayhem, & Magical Love*. In 2021, Sola married the woman who inspired the Allison Tinke character. He lives in Florida and is taking notes for his next writing project.

THE $HOW
LAWRENCE H. SOLA

NOTE FROM LAWRENCE H. SOLA

Word-of-mouth is crucial for any author to succeed. If you enjoyed *The Monster, Mayhem, & Magical Love*, please leave a review online—anywhere you are able. Even if it's just a sentence or two. It would make all the difference and would be very much appreciated.

Thanks!

Lawrence H. Sola

We hope you enjoyed reading this title from:

www.blackrosewriting.com

Subscribe to our mailing list – *The Rosevine* – and receive **FREE** books, daily deals, and stay current with news about upcoming releases and our hottest authors.
Scan the QR code below to sign up.

Already a subscriber? Please accept a sincere thank you for being a fan of Black Rose Writing authors.

View other Black Rose Writing titles at www.blackrosewriting.com/books and use promo code **PRINT** to receive a **20% discount** when purchasing.